Cruising on ICE

Palmer City VOLTAGE
BOOK 1

KERRY EVELYN

Swan Press

Cruising on Ice by Kerry Evelyn © 2021

Edited by Nicole Ayers, Ayers Edits

Proofed by SharpEditor & BookNookNuts

Cover design and interior formatting by Chris Kridler, Sky Diary Productions

Paperback ISBN: 978-1-7361977-7-6

Printed in the United States of America

First Printing: August 2021 Swan Press

To Coach Carrie and Coach Caleb,
for teaching my kids what matters most:
believing in yourself, loving what you do,
working hard, having integrity,
and catching others before they hit the ground.

And to those struggling with self-worth:
YOU ARE GOOD ENOUGH.
Read that again.

TAYLOR

"Go, go, go! Charge up, Voltage!" Less than ten seconds on the clock. I would have held my breath if I hadn't needed it to scream.

My favorite player and the best guy I knew, Kingston Brewer, broke free of the opposing defensemen as the puck sailed toward him from across the ice. The beating in my chest accelerated like a drumroll as I flattened my hands against the Plexiglas. His right hand slid down the stick as he brought it back for a slap shot.

"You got this!" I shrieked. "Give 'em a Brews-ing!" The black rubber disk made contact with the tape on his wooden stick. It whizzed over the goalie's shoulder and into the back of the net. I threw my arms in the air as the red light flashed and the horn sounded, signaling the end of the second overtime period.

I leapt onto my seat and yanked the pom-pom of my knit hat so I could throw it over the glass. A flock of caps flew toward the ice to celebrate his hat trick. Hockey was full of fun traditions, and this one never got old.

As his teammates skated toward him, Kingston looked over to me. His brother and I were watching at ice level, next to the Palmer City Voltage's penalty box. Our eyes connected, and he winked, sending those butterflies that had made a home in my belly into a tailspin before he was tackled by Alexei Kriz, one of the team's alternate captains, and then the rest of the team.

I tried to remain cool, but his attention was a drug I would never get enough of. This Crush of All Crushes began when I first saw him. He and my sister, Chelsea, became besties their freshman year of high school. He was around. A lot. But I'd managed to avoid an introduction for months because I was an awkward sixth grader and . . . he was *not*. I could never have let on about my crush, not then and not now. The humiliation of his rejection was something I couldn't bear to face.

Over time, and with much effort, I'd perfected the art of not showing anything more than friendship toward him. I'd had to. Especially when Chelsea started dating Jackson, Kingston's older brother, and our families got connected. By the time I reached high school, Kingston had been recruited to play hockey for a prep school, and I spent most of those years pining for him and dating guys who never measured up.

It'd been easy to be friends with him when he moved back home to play for Palmer City's minor-league team. Safe, even. My unrequited crush was always doomed to go unnoticed while he still thought of me as the little sister he never had. And it wasn't like he would be introduced to any other perspective while in our small town. In a lot of ways, everyone treated me as the runt of the litter growing up. My small frame, high-pitched voice, and preference to hang out with Chelsea and her friends over my own peers made me the adorable and somewhat annoying tagalong of the neighborhood.

When we got older, Kingston was one of the few people who did take me seriously on occasion. In the middle of a late-night talk after Chelsea and Jackson had fallen asleep in front of the movie we were watching, we recognized that my psychology training and extensive knowledge of his background made me his ideal mindset coach—and he realized just how desperately he needed one. When I stepped into that role, I was a different Taylor Ranford in his eyes—intelligent, disciplined, perceptive, and most importantly, effective.

But still not a love interest.

"YEAAAAAAAAAAAAAAAAH!" I screamed as forcefully as my throat would allow, throwing my hands in the air and then reaching for Jackson.

He had tears in his eyes as he engulfed me in a bear hug. "They did it!"

"*He* did it!" I corrected, laughing. I fixed my gaze on the ice, where Kingston had all but disappeared under his team after scoring the winning goal of the championship series.

Jackson set me down and turned back toward the celebration below, no doubt looking for my sister while I high-fived everyone around me. He and Chelsea were back together after breaking up while he was at med school. Chelsea had moved back to town last summer to coach at our all-star cheer gym, where I taught preschoolers the basics of tumbling. She also moonlighted as one of the Voltage's spirit-squad members.

When they announced the three stars of the game, Kingston was number two, just behind the goalie. I was so incredibly proud of him. He skated to the center of the rink to thunderous applause and screaming. I'd need to drink some lemon tea tonight if I wanted to have a voice tomorrow.

"C'mon." Jackson took my arm and reached for my bag. "Let's grab my family and see if we can get down to the ice." Their parents, Mr. and Dr. Brewer, liked to watch the games from Dr. Brewer's corporate box. Tonight, their whole family had crammed into the suite. Jackson and I had popped in between periods, but we didn't stay since we both preferred to watch the game from his seats at the glass.

We rushed up the steps and onto the concourse, where we almost collided with the entire Brewer family. Aunts, uncles, cousins, grandparents—they'd all come out to see this game.

"Good, you're already here. Let's go!" Jackson nodded at his parents and dashed toward the elevator that would take us back down to the ice. I exchanged a shrug with Dr. Brewer and we followed. I wondered if Jackson's urgency was fueled more by pride for his brother or excitement to see my sister.

I finger-combed my hair absently as I thought about how far Kingston had come in the past year, both with his mindset and his game. When the third-line left winger for the Denver Edge, the Voltage's NHL affiliate, had broken his hand, they'd needed to pull someone up, and they chose Kingston. He went on to play or suit up for more games than I could count. We spoke or texted—every day—about his goals, mindset, and the daily happenings in our lives. Before every game, no matter where we were or what time of day it was, I gave him a pep talk.

When the Edge player returned just before the playoffs, Denver sent Kingston back down. It was a blow, especially when the Edge didn't qualify. Many commentators speculated that they might have advanced if Kingston had stayed with the team.

We worked through it, though. My unofficial client stepped back into his starting-line role effortlessly and led his team to the cup. His hat trick tonight was icing on the cake. This ending was possibly the best any minor league athlete could aspire to and should prove to Kingston, beyond a doubt, that he was worthy of a spot on an NHL team.

By the time we pushed through the crowd and arrived at the ice door, all the players had taken their victory laps with the cup and were now posing for a team photo. They nudged Kingston to the front, although he seemed reluctant to pose. He'd always been a humble guy. Part of that came from him thinking he was never good enough.

He was a straight-up star. I was used to second-guessing myself because other people were always doubting what I could do, but Kingston? And in a way, coaching him helped me coach myself. My brain started believing the things it heard me say, and at his suggestion, I tried out for and made the national cheerleading team. I still couldn't believe it.

The next several minutes were a blur as the team finished their celebration on the ice and headed to the locker room. I was glad they'd won the championship cup but sad the season was over.

Going to college so close to home had its perks, one of which was being able to come to all the games to see my sister and Kingston. I had loved reconnecting with him this year and hanging out, and the summer months of no hockey games coming up were already making me feel lonely for our pregame pep talks. And I'd miss the Gummi Bears he always had for me as compensation. They were my vice. He even picked out the yellow and clear ones so I wouldn't have to. Sometimes I drove to Denver with Jackson when Kingston was playing for the Edge, and he would sneak out of the locker room so we could do our pep talks in person instead of via video chat. Seeing him suited up always stirred those fluttery butterflies. There was nothing more manly or protective to me than Kingston bulked up in all that gear, flashing me a devastating smile of gratitude.

Stop it, Taylor. You're friends. You'll still see him around. Think about your birthday cruise instead. Day after tomorrow, you and Chelsea will take that sisters vacation you've been planning forever to celebrate your graduation and you making the US national cheer team.

There was that. Three weeks from now, I'd be in Florida performing at the International Cheerleading Championship. The timing had worked out perfectly, leaving one week between the end of hockey season and the start of full-team competition practices.

I think I was possibly more excited for the cruise than I was for the International Cheerleading Championship, the ultimate culmination of my cheerleading career. In part because Chelsea and I had never been on one before. I was especially excited about the pirate theme. It'd been a blast putting my costume together.

"Taylor!"

I jerked my head up when Jackson tugged my elbow. He held up his phone. "Chels said King has interviews. We should meet them in the family lounge."

"Okay."

I shot the ice a parting glance. Littered with blue, silver, black, and gold streamers and other fan fare, it was a visual reminder of the Voltage's perseverance. They'd been in last place for most of the season, barely earning a spot in the play-offs. And that was all thanks to Kingston's record-breaking goal scoring after the NHL team sent him back. I had pushed him not to think negatively of the demotion and just to take charge of what he could control.

And boy, could he control that puck!

The lounge was already bustling when we arrived. Jackson followed me over to a television monitor in the corner. On the screen, a few players sat at a table, answering questions from the media.

Kingston was doing the majority of the talking. His scruffy playoff beard and longer-than-usual hair just added to his hotness score. I smiled up at the screen with so much pride for my friend. He didn't usually enjoy giving interviews, so the journalists were taking advantage of the opportunity. I felt bad for the other players on the panel, especially the captain, goalie Jason Dexter, who'd broken the team's all-time record tonight for saves in a single game. The Madison Muskrats had shown up to play and had gone down fighting.

Kingston laughed at a reporter who asked him what had been the catalyst that kicked him into such high gear after being sent back down for the remainder of the season.

"Easy, Adri," he said to the reporter, leaning in, his expression becoming serious. "I got myself a mindset coach. It's a total game-changer."

My jaw fell to the floor.

Jackson squeezed my shoulder. "He's talking about you, you know."

"Shh!" I shushed him as the reporter asked him more about me.

"Her name?" His smile grew. "Taylor Ranford. But I'm not sure she's taking clients right now."

I pressed my hand to my forehead and grimaced, thoroughly embarrassed. "Heck no, I'm not taking clients! I don't have a certificate. I haven't even chosen a graduate program." I whisper-shouted at the screen. "Jax, what is he doing?"

Jackson draped an arm around my shoulders and grinned. "Giving credit where it's due. Admit it, Taylor, you're the reason his whole game changed. Whether you're a certified sports psychologist yet or not, he and the team have you to thank for this victory."

"That can't be true." My cheeks burned. I'd started "coaching" Kingston when I saw similar signs in him that my old teammate, Nya, had exhibited when she faced the end of her athletic career. I couldn't stand by and let him spiral downward. Back then, if I'd had my current skills, I might have been able to help her, too.

"You know it is. Don't start doubting that you're good enough. You know, you and my brother have a lot in common. You're amazing at encouraging others but underestimate your own abilities."

A wave of overwhelm hit me like a brick to my chest. I was always complaining I wasn't "seen" by others, and now Kingston had thrown me in front of the curtain on a stage I wasn't prepared to perform on.

But Jackson had a point. I was good at helping others because I'd experienced self-doubt myself. Imposter syndrome was something I'd always struggled with, and helping Kingston process it had helped me, too.

I extracted myself from Jackson's arm and walked back into the throng of people to wait for our siblings. I wanted to leave as soon as I gave Chelsea a hug and congratulated Kingston. I didn't want to be cornered by teammates—or, God forbid, the press—about mindset coaching. My sixty credits of undergraduate psychology classes in no way qualified me to be a counselor.

The spirit squad burst into the room and made a pom-pom tunnel for the players. As soon as Chelsea's arms dropped, Jackson made a beeline for her, lifting her off the ground in a hug that made me want to smile and roll my eyes at the same time. I stood back so I wouldn't get kicked by her flailing legs and scanned for Kingston.

"Baby, you're burning up," I heard Jackson say as Kingston found their family. I looked on with a smile when his parents started crying. They waved me over, but even though they considered me part of their family, I didn't want to intrude on that emotional moment.

Waitasecond.

Chelsea was burning up?

Was she sick?

No, no, no, no, no, no. She was not allowed to be sick. We were boarding a plane tomorrow afternoon.

I closed the few feet between us. "Chels, are you okay?" When she turned her face, I saw it in her eyes. Makeup couldn't hide everything.

Oh no!

She avoided my gaze.

My heart thudded in panic, and I forced a smile. "I'm sure it's just the excitement."

We were both really looking forward to this sister bonding time. It had to be something a good night's sleep could fix.

"I don't think so." Her lash extensions drooped, and she leaned on Jackson. "I ache all over."

"Aw, baby. Let me get you home," Jackson said. "Taylor, you should stay and go on to the party. I can take care of her."

I inhaled deeply, scrunching up my shoulders in frustration. "Yes. Fine. Okay. But you have to get better, Chels! We fly out tomorrow, and it would stink to be sick on the ship."

"I don't think you're getting on a plane tomorrow, babe," Jackson whispered to her. He looked at me. "Can't you rebook?"

"No, we cannot rebook." My voice rose in volume, and I cringed, blinking at him and hating my voice. I sounded like a little kid. Why would anyone ever take me seriously?

But was *he* serious? I loved Jackson and all, and he was normally a smart man—a doctor like his mother—but when it came to my sister, he was often just plain dumb. I gaped at him. "There's no other time to rebook! Even if we could, which we can't, because of the cancellation policy."

I started to pace. I'd really been looking forward to this trip. I knew it wasn't Chelsea's fault she was sick, but why did it have to happen now, of all times?

"I have to report for competition in a week. And I still need to finalize a graduate program and find an assistantship. Hopefully one that pays, because coaching preschoolers barely covers the bills." I was losing my cool for sure. And I hated that. I knew my sister would feel bad about missing the trip, and my rant was likely making her feel worse. All the stress of this gap semester was boiling up to the surface.

Jackson chewed his lip. "You could bring a friend?"

"Jax," I said as calmly as I was able. "Who's available the night before? I'll just have to go by myself!" I threw up my hands and spun on my heel, crashing straight into the wall that was Kingston's hard chest.

Oh, lord, *that face.* His concerned expression shot me through the heart, and I fought back tears as the heat spreading across my cheeks burned into my soul like a five-alarm fire, complete with sirens ringing in my ears.

Maybe I'd caught Chelsea's cruddy cold. That had to be it, because I didn't want to even think about the other reason.

"Hey, Lorikeet." His arms shot out to steady me. "Yikes, what'd they say to get you so mad? Where are you going?"

"I'm not a bird. And God help you if you tell me *one more time* that I'm cute when I'm mad!" I raised myself to my full five feet three inches—in shoes—and thumbed my hand in my sister's direction. I regretted the poor choices of my eleven-year-old self, who wanted to go by Lori because the mean middle school girls told me that Taylor was a boy's name and didn't match my baby voice. I wish I'd never let even one mean girl get to me all those years ago.

Kingston could never seem to remember Lori, and he went through several ridiculous nicknames before settling on Lorikeet, Tay-lo being the worst. I shuddered. The nickname was worse than my real name, but it stuck, unlike Lori, which no one except Chelsea had ever called me. And she only did it to make me feel better.

Worst of all, Lorikeet reminded me that I hated my voice. Kingston had no idea the extent to which the nickname's roots bothered me, and I had no plans to tell him. At least he purposely didn't try to be mean about it.

"Taylor." He cupped my shoulders and forced me to look at him. "Hold on. Where are you going by yourself?"

"My birthday cruise!" Salty tears stung my eyes, threatening to spill. I felt terrible that Chelsea was sick, but . . . I *needed* this trip. I needed a reset. I needed to have fun without the pressures of real life. "I know I shouldn't complain. Chelsea's too sick to travel tomorrow. I—I'm going to have to go by myself or cancel."

Kingston looked past me. Maybe he'd think Chelsea wasn't as sick as Jackson thought. Doctors are super cautious by design, and Jackson was no exception. Kingston had ignored his brother's medical advice a gazillion times over the years, as many athletes and performers do. I mean, what the heck? Chelsea and I were *cheerleaders,* for goodness' sake. We'd performed and competed with the flu, severe sprains, broken bones, you name it—even pneumonia.

It was too quiet all of a sudden. No doubt Kingston and Chelsea were doing that secret BFF-Jedi-mind-trick communication stuff they'd perfected when they were in high school. I followed his gaze.

Chelsea's eyes were wide and darted from me to Kingston. "Maybe Kingston could go with you? Please, bestie? Watch over my sister and make sure she has a good birthday? Jackson can check in on your cats while you're gone."

Kingston dropped his hands from my shoulders and folded his sculpted, beefy arms across his chest. The side of his mouth turned up. Did he think this was funny?

"On the cruise? And to Disney World afterward?" I asked. "Chels, no. I'm fine, really. I'm sure he has plans—"

"Sounds fun," he said.

"No, you can't go, Kingston!" I shook my head in disbelief. As much as I would love it—*STOP, Taylor. Hasn't happened, won't happen, ain't ever going to happen.* I took a breath to steady my thoughts and turned back to my sister. "Chels, he freaking just won a championship. There'll be interviews, appearances, parades—this team hasn't won a championship in decades—the town is going to want to celebrate!"

Kingston's jolly bark of a laugh cut me off.

"What's so funny?" I furrowed my brow. "That was an incredible game. You were amazing out there. You even got a hat trick!"

"Well, thanks." Did his smile look a little sad? "But we don't get that kind of attention, Taylor, not at this level of play. Our season is over. We'll have our big celly tonight, but I'm free after that until I start coaching kids at the Plex. Hopefully, the win will entice Denver to bring me up permanently, but it's a waiting game right now." He waggled his eyebrows. "A cruise sounds fun. Plus, I like the sunshine. I haven't been on a cruise or to Disney since I played in Orlando. Fun times."

I could only blink at him. I think I moved my mouth, but nothing audible came out. Was this really happening? *Play it cool, Ranford,* I coached myself.

"Oh, that's great!" Chelsea croaked. *Huh.* She'd sounded fine ten minutes ago. "I was really nervous at the thought of her going by herself."

"Wait!" I poked Kingston in the chest. "First of all, I don't want you to come if it's only because you've got nothing better to do. Second, what was that mindset coach thing about? Don't try to distract me from that. That wasn't cool. Third, it's too late to amend the reservation without paying hefty fees."

"Hey, no, don't think that, Taylor. We'd have fun." His assurance seemed sincere, but I was skeptical. Why would he want to do this for me? He had to have better things going on this week.

"We'd all feel better that you're not going on a cruise by yourself. It's not safe," Jackson said before Kingston could address the mindset-coaching thing. "And this guy has extra cash from that sub-shop endorsement. What's that jingle again, King?"

Kingston snorted and held up a fake sub. "A Cityside sub after a night on the ice is my idea of something that's reeeeeeeeally niiice."

I rolled my eyes before pleading with my sister. "Chels, how do you know you won't be better in the morning?" I asked. "Maybe you ate something bad or—"

Chelsea's already flushed face reddened even more. "It's—"

"Sounds like bronchitis," Jackson said.

"Really." I pursed my lips.

"I can get Mom or a team doc to verify if you want," Jackson said with a shrug.

I sighed and waved my hands for emphasis, as if that would make my heart stop racing. Even thinking about Kingston being on the cruise with me made it go into overdrive. "No, it's fine. I'm so sorry you're sick, Chels. Really. I'm just . . . sad, I guess. And I know you must be, too."

"We'll plan another trip, Tay. Promise."

I nodded and turned back to Kingston. "Pick me up at eleven at the gym, Brewer. Bring that snazzy suit you wore to your last away game. And you'll need a pirate costume and your skates. There's an ice rink on the ship."

I turned so abruptly, my sneakers squeaked on the floor. I had a little over twelve hours to get my head on straight. This could be the best week of my life, or the worst. There could be no in between.

"Taylor, wait!" Kingston caught up to me. "Are you going

to the after-party? We could ride together, and you can fill me in on the itinerary."

I stopped and sucked in a deep breath as he cut in front of me to open the door to the hall. Better to embrace it than to fight him. The kindness in his expression did me in, and all at once, my smile was real. Always attentive, he naturally put others at ease. That was part of the reason I'd given up trying to find anyone like him. Guys like Kingston were few, and they were usually snatched up young. "Sure, thanks. That would be great. I can't stay long, though. Early classes at the gym and all before we leave."

"Awesome. I don't want to stay long, either. Just let me get my stuff—"

A reporter shoved a microphone between us. I stepped out of the way.

"Kingston, great to catch you! Is this your Taylor? What an amazing night you had. And a great interview after the game. But you didn't mention your future plans. What are you going to do next?"

His eyes clouded briefly, and then he shot me a grin that made my knees weak. "I'm going to Disney World!"

2

KINGSTON

I'm going to Disney World? What a lame thing to say. Taylor's twitching lips confirmed it.

Adri Delicata ate it up, though. She wasn't just any sports reporter; she was a hockey fanatic who watched the peewees with the same fervor as the pros. With two sons playing college hockey, she was more than a fan.

"Disney World, hmm?" She narrowed her eyes, but a smile played at her lips. "I hadn't heard news of the team sponsoring such an event."

I squared my shoulders and nodded to Taylor. "She's gonna perform out there. You are looking at Team USA Cheer's newest basket girl."

Taylor's lips parted in surprise. I hoped it was okay talking about her. I didn't want to discuss my lack of a contract for next season.

Adri's eyes sparkled. "That's a long way to go to support your *mindset coach.* Are you dating?"

Her direct question caught me off guard, and I laughed

nervously. "Nah. She's my best friend's little sister. We've been buds since she was a kid. Like family."

"Mm-hmm." Adri's eyes darted between us, and Taylor shifted from foot to foot, her gaze fixed on the door. I needed to wrap this up.

I told Adri most of what she wanted to hear, and Taylor answered a few questions about our pregame pep talks. When Adri finally cut us loose, I took Taylor's hand and playfully tugged her down the hall. "Let's go before more of them find me."

She did that pulling-her-lips-into-her-mouth thing that indicated she was either thinking or stopping herself from saying something she wanted to say but probably shouldn't. I grabbed my bag, and we made our way to the lot where my SUV was parked.

"What is it?" I opened the passenger door. "Come on, tell me what's bugging you."

She slid in and looked up at me. "I'm just thinking."

It was never good when a woman said she was *just thinking*.

I closed her door and tossed my gear in the trunk, thinking about how to distract her from whatever she was *just thinking* about. I hated seeing her upset. I remembered I'd bought Gummi Bears on my way into the arena today and plucked them from my bag. I hadn't had a chance to remove the yellow and clear ones yet —she never ate those—but I thought the gesture might help.

I settled in behind the wheel and presented the bag of bears with a flourish. "Gummi Bear for your thoughts?"

She took the bag and wrinkled her nose. "You didn't de-sunshine them."

"My deepest apologies." She laughed, and I held out my palm for the rejected pineapple and lemon bears. While she piled them into my hand, I tipped my chin in her direction. It was always a conscious effort to casually inhale the orange-and-vanilla scent that emanated from her. "So hit me up with all the details. Which ship are we sailing on? Did you already choose excursions?"

Taylor popped three red bears into her mouth and closed her eyes. I watched her face as the sweet sugary treat did its magic. It worked. The sugar spike both relaxed and energized her, and she talked about the cruise for the entire duration of the drive to Brewski's Sports Bar & Grille, the team's favorite sports pub. My uncle opened the place when we kids were in elementary school, and my dad, Jackson, and I would often go there after a Voltage game. Even then, players would converge on the place after practices and games. It had always been the unofficial hangout for the team, and I'd wanted to be just like them. Most of the players went on to play for the NHL after a year or two with the Voltage, and that's what I'd been expecting, too.

I should've been over the moon to go to the after-party, drink too much, and act stupid with my teammates. But all I could think about was how I'd already spent too many years on teams at this level and my time was running out to move up. This was my third season at this level. If I was going to get a full-time NHL roster spot, it needed to happen soon, or it wouldn't ever happen. Adri's questions had reminded me how fast my career clock was ticking, and I didn't want to spend the rest of those years in the minors. Truthfully, right now, all I wanted to do was head home to book the flight and pack for this cruise.

I'd been on a similar cruise with a bunch of the guys on the Orlando team a few years ago, so I was up for whatever Taylor wanted to do. The opportunity to spend a week with her, alone, was something I was definitely looking forward to. We had an easy friendship and a history that went back over a decade. We'd always gotten along great, created fun when there wasn't any to be found, and had a similar sense of humor. We were both down on ourselves a lot and had fallen into a natural role of becoming each other's cheerleaders.

But lately, she'd started to affect me in other ways, and I wanted—no, needed—to know if that was just because of her positive encouragement and how her coaching made me feel, or if there was something more stirring on my end.

If something more was stirring, it would be smart to tamp it down ASAP. Taylor was like a sister to me, and the friend zone was the least complicated place to be. I couldn't imagine my life without her in it, and that ran me scared of asking her out as more than friends. If we ever crossed the line, there'd be no going back.

I held the door open and gestured for Taylor to go in first. The restaurant hadn't changed much since we were kids. It had been designed to fuse a traditional Irish pub with a modern brewery. Brewing equipment lined the left wall, and a snug room next to the bar afforded a larger party privacy as well as personal service.

My aunt and uncle stepped out from behind the host stand when they saw us enter. I grinned. They'd just been at the game. I waved to my cousins: Drew, behind the bar, and Brenna, who was waiting for him to add drinks to a tray she held. "Already back to work?"

"Always work to be done!" Aunt Angie replied. "And it's an important night."

My uncle laughed. "A small-business owner never sleeps. There's almost a hundred people in that room over there, waiting for you. Congratulationss, Kingston. We're all so incredibly proud of you."

"Aw, thanks, Uncle Quinn." I scanned the walls, peppered with sports equipment and memorabilia, including my framed Voltage jersey, hanging in a prominent spot, replacing previous jerseys as I'd moved up the ranks. I'd never seen my family so excited as when I got traded home, and I knew they were hoping for a Denver Edge jersey to replace this one. They'd kept the function room empty tonight in the event we won.

We stopped briefly at a large table to greet my parents, who sat with members of the medical team, and continued on to the function room. Most of the guys were already there celebrating when we entered. Taylor ducked behind me as they cheered my arrival.

"Bruise!" I chuckled at the nickname the team had given me after my first few games. "First round on me!" Alexei pounced on me and handed me a yard glass. "Big drink for big plays!" His slurred words and heavier-than-usual Czech accent indicated he had to be a few drinks in already.

I laughed and lifted the glass to my mouth, aware of Taylor's eyes watching me.

"Tip it up!" I almost choked as Trask Emerson lifted the bottom of the glass. I chugged until he let go when the others crowded around me.

I grinned and set the glass down on the nearest table so I could high-five, hug, and back-clap the guys.

"NHL will surely bring you up now!" I smiled at Alexei's genuine comment but felt a pang of uncertainty knowing my two-way contract was up. He put his arm around me and guided me to the corner where his wife, Ginny, was sitting with Jason's girlfriend, Lauren.

"From your lips to God's ears," I said, sinking into a chair next to him. I scanned for Taylor, wondering where she'd gone. The room wasn't that big.

There.

My eyes narrowed as I spotted her with Trask and a couple newer members of the team. I always kept my eye on her when she was around the players; she was too good to waste her time with half these guys. No, most of these guys. Minor leaguers were especially transient. They'd love her and leave her when they got traded or brought up and never give her a second thought. Trask would look out for her, so I relaxed into the booth. He was a good guy, and though newer to the team, he'd been named the second alternate captain this season.

"You look the opposite of how someone who just won a championship should look," Ginny observed. "Are you planning to rip out your teammates' throats, or am I misreading your expression?"

"Huh?" Where was my beer? I poured a glass of water from the pitcher in the middle of the table and took a sip.

She laughed. "Never mind. Great game tonight."

"Thanks."

"Delivery for Kingston Brewer!" I looked up. The new server, Kami, stood in the doorway holding a huge box.

Trask pushed a few guys out of the way to help her. The

transfer was slightly off balance and awkward, and as soon as Trask had a good hold of the box, Kami rushed back out.

"Cityside Subs sends their best!" He dropped the box on a table and followed Kami out of the room. I wondered what that was about. Trask was naturally a polite guy, but he'd seemed extra attentive to Kami since she'd started working here.

The guys pounced on the subs, even though the restaurant had set out a buffet. My thoughts returned to my prospects, and suddenly, I wasn't hungry or in the mood to celebrate. My agent hadn't called or texted, except for a short *Great game, kid!* There wasn't any of the buzz I'd expected, even after playing the best game of my professional career and all the local media attention.

It was probably better for everyone if I headed home to sulk. I didn't want to bring the mood down, especially for the younger guys who'd never won a championship before. I circled the room, keeping Taylor in my peripheral vision until I reached her.

"Hey, you." I didn't have to fake a smile for her. I loved that she wore the jersey I gave her. Even if she wouldn't let me sign it until I "made it big." She had so much faith in me. Her limitless confidence always made me feel like I could take on the world. Trouble was, I always came up short. Even tonight.

I often made jokes about being second best. Jackson had been class president and was now a doctor. My teammates outscored me by a goal or two and clinched records. I'd been passed over for leadership roles more times than I could count. But I'd always been a team player and a hard worker, even when I wasn't living up to my own expectations. Taylor was the only one who knew it bothered me, and we'd spent the beginning of the season working on my self-esteem.

"Hey, there you are. I was just about to look for you," Taylor said.

"You were?" My chest warmed.

"Yeah. I have to get going. I still have a lot to get done."

"I was heading out myself. Do you—would you like me to take you home?"

She glanced toward where I'd been sitting. "Lauren said she and Jay could give me a ride, but . . ." She pressed her lips together, and I stared at them, waiting for her to finish. "If I went with you, maybe we could talk more about the trip?"

An instant smile covered my face. For a second, I thought she was going to turn my offer down. "Yeah. Let's do it."

"Great!" She brightened, and I chuckled, slinging my arm over her shoulders. We were definitely going to have a great time on the cruise, because I would do whatever it took to keep that smile on her face.

3

TAYLOR

Oh, lordy. This was too much Kingston. Too much, too much, too much.

In theory, too much Kingston was never enough. Not in my world, anyway. Not since the first time I saw him. He'd come to our house to work on a project with Chelsea when they were in ninth grade. I'd spied on them, in total awe of his easy confidence, almost-shoulder-length hair pulled under a backward ball cap, athletic build *(who had defined biceps at fourteen?)*, and Hollywood grin. I'm pretty sure I swooned upon first glance.

But too much *unstructured* Kingston was not good for my heart—or my standards for men. There just wasn't anyone else like him. I would need to plan out every minute of this cruise, because every unplanned minute left room for unplanned feelings to manifest.

When he moved back to Palmer City, it was hard to hang out with him because he viewed the trade home as a devastating setback. For someone as talented, skilled, and disciplined as Kingston, it had surprised me just how much he doubted himself. Seeing him without the confidence that made him stand out to me made my heart hurt. I had to try and help him gain it back.

The path to the NHL is different for every player, and Kingston's ride so far had been long and twisty. He'd been away from home for many years, playing for a private high school in Denver and forgoing a four-year college when he entered the draft at eighteen and was chosen by the New Orleans Crescents.

The team determined he needed more experience, and after a couple of years of junior hockey, he made a roster spot on the organization's lowest-tier professional team in Orlando. After that, he was brought up to their next-level affiliate in upstate New York, and we all thought it was just a matter of time until he was called up to the Crescents. Instead, they traded him in a deal with Denver, who sent him down to their minor league team here in our hometown of Palmer City, right outside Colorado Springs. He'd had a rocky start here, and his game suffered as his self-esteem plummeted.

I'd graduated this past December with a psychology degree, but last fall I began working with Kingston on his misbeliefs and imposter syndrome. After I started helping him, his play improved significantly, and he played well when Denver called him up.

During our "sessions," I had practiced utmost professionalism. Yes, I had supported Kingston and become his confidante and cheerleader, but there had been purpose and goals and *plans* to follow.

There had to always be a purpose, otherwise my heart would try to override my brain. I'd grasp at straws if I had to, but I would find a reason *and* a purpose for this second car ride tonight.

Sitting next to him, I couldn't get comfortable. My pony-tail felt tighter than usual, and I was fidgety. I reached up and tugged on the elastic bow to slide it down my ponytail and onto my wrist. I ran my fingers through the stiff, sprayed-back hair in an attempt to fluff it out a bit.

He was watching me.

"What?" I asked.

"You don't wear your hair down much anymore. Is that one of the bows you made?"

"It is."

"It's got a heart and a number sixteen on it."

"It does." Where was he going with this?

"It's the Voltage colors. I like it."

"It's the—" I looked at the bow. Uh-oh. *His* number was sixteen. I smirked and fought the heat warming my cheeks. "You think I made this because I fangirl you?" I poked his side, and we both grinned. "Eyes on the road, Brewer, and you can rest assured there's no need to read too deeply into it." *Crap!* Was anyone else thinking what he was thinking?

"Really?" His skeptical tone was teasing.

"Left over from a Sweet Sixteen party for one of the members of the senior all-girl team. I kept the sample because it matched my jersey."

"You mean *my* jersey."

"Not anymore. You gave it to me."

"I did." He pulled his car into my apartment complex, near the university's campus. I stared out the front window for a moment, taking in the magnificent glow of the moon. It enhanced the starlight and cast shadows from the pines and aspens onto the rocks outside my building.

So much for having a plan or purpose for the car ride.

I unbuckled my seat belt and threw open the door when he put the car in park next to mine. "Thanks for the ride, Brewer. I'll see you tomorrow."

4

KINGSTON

*P*almer City had all the charm of a small town, and technically it was, despite its name. Back in its founding days, it had more people than the average Colorado settlement, so the founders chose to call it a city. Snowpack Creek, a narrow waterway paralleling Main Street, divided the town. The gentle sound of the water rushed over and around rocks, generating a sense of calm, even on chaotic days. I grew up not far from the town line, on the north-western side of Colorado Springs, across the creek from the Arena, and not too far from the Plex, our area's one-stop multi-structure recreation complex, where the Voltage practiced and where Taylor's and Chelsea's youth cheer teams trained.

When I moved back, I decided to splurge on a gated apartment complex several of my teammates lived in, a little farther out. The amenities, including a full gym and Olympic-size indoor swimming pool, were worth the extra ten minutes in the car to get anywhere. As was the wildlife. The farther from the center of town I went, the more likely I was to see deer, wild turkey, and even an occasional elk or black bear.

As I approached the door to my apartment, I was greeted by the welcoming mewing of Luc and Bourque, my two rescue cats. My living space was over the garage, and the vibrations, when the door opened and closed, signaled to the tabbies that treats were forthcoming. "Hold on, hold on."

Hockey players have nothing on cat owners when it comes to fancy footwork. We played this game every time I got home; they wove in between and around my legs, begging for treats, and I concentrated on staying upright long enough to drop my bag and pull out the end table drawer that contained said treats.

I sank into the couch, treats in hand, and they were on my lap before my backside made contact with the cushions. "Good game tonight, guys. You should've been there." I poured a few treats in my hand. Two wet noses tickled my palm as they made short work of them. "I scored a hat trick. My last goal was at the horn, and it won the game for us. We got the cup."

Luc nudged Bourque off my lap, turned in a circle, and plopped down, facing the TV. Bourque, ever the submissive one, tucked in at my side. I scratched them both between their ears. "Yeah, so that's a big deal in my world. All the fans throw their hats onto the ice for the hat trick. And there's a big trophy. Anyway, I should also mention I'll be leaving for a week or so. Uncle Jackson will keep you fed and clean your litter till I get back."

Neither cat responded, of course. I gently lifted the trying-to-sleep Luc off my lap and placed him on the cushion next to Bourque. Tonight, I'd book a flight to Orlando, rent a pirate costume, and pack. Tomorrow, I'd get a haircut and shave, pick up the costume, and meet Taylor after her morning tumbling classes.

I closed my eyes and smiled, thinking of her. Smart, fierce, determined, and dedicated to helping others. I felt bad that the one thing she was doing for herself—the cruise—wasn't going as planned, but I was looking forward to making sure it turned out better than she expected.

THE NEXT MORNING I DROVE AROUND THE PLEX TO THE CHEER gym's parking lot, arriving a few minutes after eleven. Kids and moms were filing out as I set my vehicle in park. I locked it and jogged up the stairs to the entrance. I'd been here a few times for events, so I knew where to look for Taylor. As I neared the end of the hall that led to the main cheer floor, I heard her counting in the light but firm voice that made people want to listen.

I loved her voice. It was little and cute, like her. Not a mean note to be heard, even when she was upset or angry—or both, like last night when she learned it wouldn't be the sister cruise she and Chelsea had been planning practically their whole lives. Jackson had texted that Chelsea was even sicker this morning and felt even worse that she couldn't go.

Rounding the corner, I stopped short at the pause in Taylor's counting. Her brawny stunt partner, Nate, held her by her feet, with his arms extended above his head. I'd never admit it out loud, but I was a little jealous of the man who'd gotten to pick her up and toss her around for the last five years. They had a close friendship and could feel and adjust to each other in a way that was similar to how I communicated with my teammates on the ice. I wondered if Taylor trusted me the way she trusted Nate. I leaned against the wall to watch.

"One more time all the way through, Tay, and I think we're good." His deep voice was the ultimate contrast to hers, and it ruffled me that he shortened her name. I narrowed my eyes at him as she transitioned down to the floor.

"Let's do it." Her back was to me, and when her hands slapped to her sides for her starting position, I froze. "Set. Five, six, seven, eight . . ."

Her shorts were *short*. Like competition-uniform short. I didn't know why, all of a sudden, I noticed—really noticed—or why it bugged me. I'd seen her—and other athletes—in short shorts before. But I couldn't pull my eyes away, even though I knew I should. She was my best friend's little sister. It was just protective instincts, right?

Nate bent at the knees as Taylor began with a handstand. He caught her feet and bounced her upward until she was standing with her feet together in his right hand. A series of flips and tosses followed. Up, around, down, back up again, kicking out, twisting. *Wow.* I wondered if there was anything Taylor couldn't do.

He caught her in his arms, groom-style, and she bounced to the floor, finally noticing I was there. "You're late, Brewer!"

I lifted my bare wrist to pretend to check the time. "Sorry, forgot my watch."

She snorted as she walked toward me. "Aw, you got a haircut. It's nice, but I think I miss the long, scraggly helmet hair." She reached up to run her fingers through the cropped curls on the top of my head and then patted them into place. "And you shaved your playoff beard." As her finger grazed my now baby-soft cheek, our eyes connected and I held my breath. My skin burned in the wake of her caress. She cleared her throat. "You know Nate, right?"

I swallowed. "It's been a while." Taylor scooted to the side, and I held out my hand.

"Good to see you," Nate said, pulling me into a bone-crushing bear hug. "Congrats on the win last night. Awesome hat trick. My roommate and I are big fans."

"Thanks, man." I coughed and he finally let go. "You ready, Lorikeet?"

She rolled her eyes. "Yeah. I've just got to get my stuff out of the coaches' room."

Nate slapped a hand on my shoulder. I didn't flinch, but man, was that force necessary? I looked up at him. "You take care of her, you hear? She said she plans to party, but sometimes she doesn't recognize her limits." He flicked a concerned glance toward her. "Know what I mean?"

I didn't, not really, but he sounded serious. "No worries, man. She's family. No one shady will get near her with me around."

He studied me for a second, and I felt like he was assessing my worthiness as a protector. "Good. She's worked too hard to lose focus or get distracted this week. The only reason I'm going to this international comp is because she wants me to. It's the only title she doesn't have, and if we can outperform Canada, it's in the bag. *If* all of our athletes remain mentally, physically, and *emotionally* strong."

"Don't see any reason why that would change," I said. But I felt Nate's eyes on me as I followed Taylor to get her stuff. I took a giant suitcase in each hand while she pulled a hoodie over her head and slung her backpack over her shoulder. I raised my eyebrows when she finally looked at me.

"It's not all for the cruise, just so you know. I'm also taking all the stuff I'll need in Orlando to prep for the cheer championship."

"It's all good. You sure you don't need more stuff? Coffee maker, kitchen sink?" I teased.

She wrinkled her nose. "Funny."

I followed her out of the building and into the parking lot, trying to keep my eyes above her waist. I was pretty sure the airlines had rules about shorts that short, and for good reasons.

Guys like me being one of them. I couldn't stop looking.

"Stop staring at my butt," she called back to me, flashing a grin over her shoulder.

Busted. "I was just thinking you look kinda chilly. You need to borrow some pants for the flight?"

She snorted and patted her backpack. "Don't worry, *Dad*. I'll put on pants before I sit with strangers on the plane."

"Yeah, about that. I couldn't get Chelsea's seat, but there are a few open spots in first class. You wanna upgrade?"

She didn't answer right away. "How much?"

I shrugged. "I'll take care of it." Her, too. And not because Nate or Chelsea or Jackson wanted me to.

Because *I* wanted to.

5

TAYLOR

First class was pretty nice, but the accommodations weren't as luxurious as I'd imagined. The seats were wider, and they served complimentary drinks; however, I still had to share the armrest.

I had to admit, I was a little nervous about traveling with Kingston. I'd been planning to use the time seated apart to get my mind set and make more plans to keep us busy.

And now we were sitting together.

Kingston gave me the choice of window or aisle, and I chose the window seat. I'd settled as close to the side of the plane as possible, pulling my legs up and crossing them with my body facing the aisle—and Kingston. Unexpected shyness had set in, and I wasn't ready to be shoulder-to-shoulder with him.

The gym's branded warm-up pants I'd thrown in my bag weren't the best choice of bottoms, since they lacked pockets, but they were comfortable and got Kingston off my back.

Well, as comfortable as they could be for legs that were cramping up and pins-and-needly. After about twenty minutes sitting with my legs crossed, my muscles were screaming for oxygen and movement.

The flight attendants finished their spiel, and I eyed the armrest that separated us. The entire length of it was covered by his shapely forearm, lightly dusted with blond hair. His biceps and triceps were hardly contained by a short-sleeved dry-fit polo shirt.

"Are you staring at my muscles?" He held up his arm and flexed.

Busted. I rolled my eyes to mask my embarrassment.

"I, ugh . . . can I use the armrest? I can't seem to get comfortable."

His lips twitched, but he moved his arm. I took a deep breath, placed a hand on each armrest, and twisted my body toward the seat in front of me. I pushed down, which raised me up off the seat, and willed my legs to unfold. They did, begrudgingly, and I lowered myself back into the seat with a sigh of relief, pointing and flexing my feet to stretch out my aching calves. I reached down to massage them and felt his eyes on me.

"Leg cramp? You okay? Need some water?"

"I'm good, thanks." I finished rubbing life into my legs and buckled up. "Are you planning to stare at me the entire flight?"

Kingston winced, and I felt bad. That probably sounded harsh.

"Sorry. You just seem on edge? You're usually calm and relaxed."

And I'm not usually forced to go on vacation and share a tiny space with a man I've crushed on for years, so yeah, I'm a little on edge.

I couldn't say that, though.

"Just sore from my workout, I guess. Nate came in before my classes, and we hit it hard for a while. Then I showered and taught my littles. When you were late, we practiced a bit more. It was probably too much." I pulled my water out of the seat-back pocket and took a long drink.

"You and Nate looked really good this morning. I think it's cool that you both made the national team. You're amazing to watch."

His comment made me feel all warm and fuzzy, and I couldn't stop the huge smile that spread across my face.

"I'm glad his schedule allowed for it this year. It's something I've always wanted to do." I'd competed on championship college and Worlds teams, but the national team was something totally different. Even the best of the best had a hard time getting a spot because there were only so many roles to fill and only seven females on the mat. I'm short, so I fly in the co-ed division. My roommate, Kaycee, is tall. She's been on the all-girl national team for three years and encouraged me to try out one more time. I'd never have made it on my own. But when Nate and I tried out as partners this year, they took us both.

"I remember."

"You do?" That surprised me. When had we talked about this? Our conversations were usually about hockey or our siblings.

"When I first met you." He grinned at the memory. "You weren't cheering yet. You told me you wanted to be on the US women's gymnastics team." He half smiled, eliciting the dimple in his left cheek.

I groaned and covered my face with my hand. Though I'd first glimpsed him when I was eleven, I'd avoided every opportunity to speak with him—until we officially "met" at my twelfth birthday party at the Plex's public skating rink. I fell, and he skated over to pull me up. Chelsea had invited him to help the girls who couldn't skate. Funny how even my friends who could skate had trouble that day. I was skinny, short, had braces, and wished I was cooler and prettier, like my sister, who brought home super cute study partners she had no romantic interest in.

Well, just *one* super cute study partner.

He made me nervous, so whenever we had to talk, I always ran my mouth about gymnastics because I didn't have to think about it.

"Hey," he said, pulling my hand away from my face. "Nothing to be embarrassed about. You were fierce and confident. You told me it didn't matter if you couldn't skate because you could tumble. Why'd you stop gymnastics, anyway?"

My eyes slitted and I pressed my lips together. I wasn't going to tell him about Mean McKayla. He'd think I was weak. So I gave him the same line I'd given my parents. "I saw how much Chels loved cheer. Not just for school, but the All-Star competitions." I shrugged. "Less pressure, and I had a leg up because I could tumble. It was easy for me."

"And now you tumble in the air. The circus performers ain't got nothin' on Taylor Ranford and Nate Dufort." I got a full smile from him then.

"Yeah, if I don't get my master's, I can always go to Vegas," I half joked.

His grin faded to his serious face. God, he was so handsome. And a hometown celebrity. There was a reason that girls all over town stole the Cityside Subs menus with his face on them and that someone—*or someones*—had even snuck onto a billboard platform to spray-paint hearts onto the sign all around his head. Kingston brushed it off, but I knew the attention helped to build his confidence. I encouraged him to stop and sign autographs whenever someone recognized him.

I swallowed and tried to think of something to say to keep the conversation light before he could comment.

Nothing. All blank. I could only stare into his pretty blue eyes.

"It'll happen, Taylor. You told me you've already gotten accepted into three programs. Just pick one."

"Likely, I'll go with Denver since it's close to home and has what I need. It's a great program, and I can get an assistantship. It makes the most sense when I look at all my options, so I'm planning to send them my deposit after the cruise." He made it sound so easy. "And it will save me gas money, since you'll be there playing for the Edge."

He frowned when I mentioned the Voltage's affiliate team, and I wondered if he was doubting himself again. Sometimes it didn't matter how hard you worked; it mattered if you had something to offer. If you fit.

I was looking for a fit, too. No matter how smart I was, I didn't have the money just yet to fund a master's program. I'd narrowed it down to two, one out of state that was my dream program and a decent one in Denver. Close to home, cheaper, and it offered opportunities for assistantships.

This vacation was a graduation/birthday gift from my parents and grandparents. I didn't want them to have to worry about my finances when they could be enjoying their retirement. They'd worked second jobs to make sure Chelsea and I didn't have any student-loan debt or car payments, and it was my turn to pull my weight. Chelsea had funded her own master's degree, and I could, too.

Since I'd graduated in December, I'd been working more hours at the gym and creating hair bows for cheerleaders to accessorize their ponytails in my free time. My little side hustle made decent money, but it was inconsistent and mostly seasonal.

Taking this past semester off had seemed like a good idea, especially since it made me available for the national team, but I hadn't banked as much money as I'd hoped. Yet I didn't want to wait any longer. I could have attended school part-time, but I was impatient. I wanted full-time so I could finish sooner, and get my doctorate before I had kids.

Not that I was planning that anytime soon, but what almost-twenty-three-year-old doesn't think about those things? I wanted to fall in love and have babies. Babies who would grow to become bundles of personality and sass like the preschoolers I coached. I loved them, but I needed to focus on my career first to reach my ultimate goal—to support athletes through their toughest years, and then help them find a new purpose after they'd finished competing in their sport. I wanted to model a natural path that could be followed by any athlete moving into the next stage of their life.

I shot him a grateful smile as I plugged my earbuds into my phone and settled back into my seat for takeoff. I'd splurged on a few sports memoirs for this trip, and as much as I wanted to spend the next three and a half hours chatting with Kingston, I was nervous, too. After all this time coaching him and getting to know him at his deepest levels, my feelings had grown way past friendship and crushing. I was sure we could be good together, in every way. But I didn't know how to break through the friend zone we'd established, and I certainly wasn't going to risk losing him if it didn't work out. Listening to my favorite gymnast tell her story and give advice should be enough of a distraction.

6

KINGSTON

e grabbed a quick dinner in the terminal, and then headed down to the baggage claim area. I hired a limo to bring us from the airport in Orlando to the hotel in Port Canaveral. It might have been a little too much, but it was Taylor's birthday week, and I wanted to do everything I could to make up for the change of plans. The expression on her face when she saw our names on a sign held by the tux-clad driver in baggage claim was worth every cent of the Cityside Subs endorsement check I spent on it.

"This is soooo nice," she said, leaning back into the leather seats. "When you're a rich NHL player, you can travel like this all the time."

"Maybe." I deflected my gaze to the window, but I wasn't quick enough.

"Still nothing from your agent?"

I shook my head. "Let's not talk about me. This is your birthday cruise, Lorikeet."

"We have to talk about it sometime," she replied softly. "You're clearly upset, and this is what I'm here for."

"I know, and I appreciate it."

She moved to sit next to me and leaned her head on my shoulder. The simple gesture of support reminded me how lucky I was to be her friend. Joining her on the cruise was the least I could do to repay her for what she'd done for my career and my self-esteem.

We sat like that for the remainder of the ride to the hotel at the port. When the limo pulled up in front of the hotel, Taylor sat up and reached for her tote. "Why don't you check in and I'll take care of our stuff?" I suggested.

She slung the bag over her shoulder and nodded. "Cool. I'll meet you inside." The driver opened the door. I watched her go until I couldn't see her ponytail bouncing anymore. Today, she was wearing a red-and-white striped bow with a sparkly blue anchor shape in the center. I went in to get a luggage cart, helped load it, and tipped the driver.

Taylor appeared at my side. "Room two oh seven," she said, and I followed her to the elevators.

We rode up in comfortable silence. With Taylor, I didn't feel like I had to try to make conversation. We had that relaxed kind of friendship where we could be quiet together and it wasn't awkward. I thought, deep down, we were both introverts at heart. Our professions and life experiences required us to talk to people and mingle, but it had to be on our terms.

I followed her to our room. She held the door open while I pulled the cart in. As I unloaded it, she went to the window and pulled back the curtain to reveal twilight setting in over our view of the parking lot.

Taylor dropped her backpack onto the bed closest to the bathroom. "Thanks for unloading. I'll return the cart. I want to pick up some of those anti-nausea bracelets I saw in the sundries shop next to the front desk, just in case."

"Probably a good idea, being your first cruise and all."

I decided to take a quick shower to rinse off the traveling germs while she ran downstairs. I was pulling on sweatpants when the outside door clicked open. I gathered my clothes and toiletries and reentered the main room.

Taylor sat in the desk chair, scrolling on her phone. "You all set in there, Brewer? All squeaky clean?" She didn't glance up, so I dropped my things on the other bed and snuck up behind her.

"You tell me." I shook my hair out, flinging water droplets all over her.

Her squeal was worth it. "Stop!" But she laughed, so I didn't. Her phone fell into her lap, and she grabbed my head with both of her hands.

We froze, and our eyes locked for the second time today. I could hear the pounding of my heart in the silence. We were quiet just a second too long before she laughed and patted my head. "Good doggie. So clean! Now go lay down."

"Woof!" I barked, and the awkwardness seemed to lift. I lay on the bed, as instructed, and watched her as she riffled through one of her suitcases before heading to the bathroom with an armload of stuff.

A full hour later, I was sketching on my drawing pad when the buzz of the hair dryer stopped. Taylor emerged wearing a different pair of supershort shorts and my T-shirt. I frowned. I didn't remember leaving it in the bathroom.

"You should really do a better job cleaning up your mess, Brewer. I finds, I keeps. Happy birthday to me!"

"So, what you're saying is, if I want it back, I have to extract it from you?" I raise an eyebrow suggestively.

"Don't even try it, roomie," she warned, but I saw the ghost of a grin she was trying to hold back.

Her lips seem extra pink after her shower, and I found myself fixated on them. "You should do a better job of remembering to bring your own clothes into the bathroom, *roomie.*"

"And *you* should put a shirt on." Avoiding my gaze, she scooted behind the bed and squatted low to pull on a pair of pants over her shorts.

"I don't sleep in a T-shirt."

"Neither do I, usually, but these are strange times, Brewer, and you are not alone. It's only fair."

For a second, I imagined her sleeping without a shirt. *Nope, don't go there. Your purpose is to look out for her.* "Then I need my shirt back." I stuck out my hand.

"Nope!" She hefted the suitcase onto the nearby bench, turned off the main light, and crawled under the covers. "Night, roomie," she said, clicking off the light between our beds and rolling over to face the wall.

"Night, Lorikeet." She made a grumbling sound. It was too dark to see the finer details of my drawing, so I moved to the armchair by the desk. I checked my phone. Still crickets from my agent. Last night I'd had the game of my career, and I'd expected a call today, even if there wasn't any news yet.

I sketched until well past midnight, working on a comic strip for Adam, a special athlete who I mentored. He'd been my buddy for almost two years now, and he loved superheroes. During one session together, he dreamed up the ultimate hockey superplayer. Adam named him Voltage Man and decided he should look like me.

Man, did my heart grow five sizes that day. In my spare time, I drew the comics in a seven-by-ten-inch mixed-media drawing pad. Then I gave the book to Adam to read and color with whatever medium he decided to use. His occupational therapist said it was great for his fine motor control, and I could definitely say I'd seen an improvement.

I didn't want to disturb Taylor with a toilet flush, so I headed downstairs to use the restroom off the lobby. When I returned, she'd kicked off all the covers and was hugging an extra pillow.

She was a cuddler.

I thought about that as I drifted off to sleep.

WHEN MY PHONE ALARM TRILLED AT 8 A.M., TAYLOR WAS already up and packing. We grabbed breakfast to go and boarded the hotel shuttle to the terminal. *The Dreamer* was one of the smaller ships in port, but I could tell Taylor was starstruck even though she tried to pull off that she was cool.

"Hey," I said after our luggage was taken from us.

"Hm?" She was still staring at the ship. "Which room do you think is ours?"

I'd spent time on the flight exploring the ship virtually, so I felt qualified to answer. I studied the starboard side. "We're closest to the back of the ship, so count one, two, three, four lifeboats. See it?" She nodded. "We're three floors above it toward the center of that bank of rooms."

"Cool," she breathed.

"Yeah." I tried to muster an encouraging smile. "I know this isn't exactly how you planned to spend your birthday week. I'm glad to be here though, honest. Are you ready to have fun?" I winked and waggled my eyebrows.

She giggled. "Yes, I most definitely am." She adjusted her backpack on her shoulder and took my hand. "Now let's *go* already!"

I snorted and let her tug me along. The *Dreamer* awaited.

7

TAYLOR

I was here, on the *Dreamer*, fulfilling my lifelong wish to traverse the ocean underneath an endless canopy of azure sky. Ridiculously giddy, I had to keep checking myself.

Kingston didn't seem to mind my rambunctiousness, though his stomach grumbled a few times. He was probably starving, but I wanted to get to the top to take pictures of the port from the highest deck before we had lunch. There were a few other ships in port larger than ours, but I liked the coziness of our vessel. Maybe we could even make some friends on this trip. I knew before I boarded that cruising wouldn't be a one-and-done for me.

"Is it okay if we splurge on lunch here by the pool, instead of going to a dining room?" I asked Kingston as I hung on to the rail. With my dark aviator sunglasses, I hoped he couldn't see the nervousness that had returned in my eyes.

I needed to look cool.

"Sure. We can go over the itinerary, too. I know you've

made plans, but we still haven't talked about what you want to do."

I studied his face, then scanned him from his sockless leather boat shoes to his tailored navy shorts, up his fitted dry-wick polo to the navy-banded straw fedora. *What I want to do.* I just about swooned right there. Maybe it was the long-time crush or the half-drunk rum runner in my hand, but— *Cool it, Ranford. It IS your birthday cruise, remember? He's just being considerate.*

Right. Must remember. We are friends. Only friends, and the glances from every woman we passed reminded me of that.

I should also drink some water before this buzz made me too loose-lipped and I said something embarrassing or bold that I'd regret.

He was probably twice the size of me. Just shy of six feet (it irked him that his stats said five-eleven when he swore he was five-eleven and three quarters) and built like an ox, he dwarfed my five-three frame. An entire rum runner was having zero effect on him.

I settled into a lounge chair and pulled up the itinerary on my tablet. "Uh-oh. I forgot about the decades party."

"What's that?"

"You know, you choose a decade and dress like you're in it."

"When is it? Maybe we can go shopping in port?"

I sighed. "Theoretically, yes, but I hadn't budgeted for yet another eighties outfit."

"Who says it has to be eighties?"

I lifted my shades and rolled my eyes at him. "Really,

Brewer? How can you not know I'm obsessed with everything eighties?"

"I say change it up. What if we . . ." He leaned in close and held up his hands for dramatic effect. I took a deep breath to inhale his aftershave. I loved how he smelled. One time, I borrowed a hoodie from him and held on to it for months. I lowered my sunglasses back into place and breathed in through my nose, hoping it wasn't obvious I was sniffing him. "Dressed for the *nineties?*"

Staring at him, I had the urge to boop him on his nose. I tapped it lightly. "No."

He caught my hand. "I see I need to try harder to convince you. Let's go back in time to pop princesses, boy bands, overalls, and plaid everything. I can totally picture you dressed up like a bubblegum star."

Kingston was still holding my hand. I'd hardly retained a word he'd said, but just then I'd have agreed to dressing like a cavewoman if he'd suggested the Stone Age.

Find words, Taylor. "Bubblegum? That's not even a thing anymore." I shook my head but couldn't help smiling. "Fine. But I know it's because you want to throw on jeans and a flannel and call it a night. Why do *I* have to get all *TRL* fancy?"

"What's *TRL?*"

I swatted him with my free hand. "You know, that MTV video countdown show from the late nineties?"

"Never heard of it." He winked at me, and I laughed. "You don't have to dress like Shakira or anything, but your eyes lit up when I mentioned the pop princess idea. Admit it."

I laughed. "Yeah, you know me so well." Our eyes locked. This was becoming a thing.

A confusing thing.

He cleared his throat and let go of my hand. I gripped the tablet and concentrated on slowing my heartbeat.

I knew him well, too. And when he cleared his throat, it was because he was nervous or wasn't sure what to say. I'd unpack that later.

A notification popped up on my screen, alerting me to a new cheer-bow order. "Gimme a sec." I tapped on it. "Holy . . ."

"What is it?" He leaned over.

"It's an order from one of the biggest gyms on the East Coast to make bows for their Nationals teams."

"What's a Nationals team?"

"There are several championships nationwide that teams need to get a bid to attend and compete. Only the best teams get to go. This gym has *eleven* teams going. It's almost three hundred bows. And they want me to *design* it!"

"Babe, that's amazing!" He pulled me into a hug, tablet and all.

OhymyGod. He just called me babe! Had he realized it?

Kingston cleared his throat and pushed back from me. Yep, he did.

"So that'll cover your tuition deposit, right?"

Let's just both ignore that happened. Sure.

I did some fast calculations. Design fee, supply fee, my time. We were looking at thirty dollars per bow. I'd make three hundred, just in case. "I'll net over two thousand dollars." *Over two thousand dollars!* My biggest order yet. "And word might spread, which could lead to more orders."

"I'm so happy for you, Taylor. When do they need them done by?"

"When? Oh no!" I closed my eyes. I wouldn't be back in time.

"What's wrong?"

"The timeline." I groaned. "I'd need to start the bows next week in order to ship them on time. All my equipment is at home."

"What kind of equipment do you need?"

"Cutting board, cutting and weeding tools, hair bands, vinyl, my vinyl cutting machine, zip ties, ribbon, glitter, setting spray, Mom's heat press—"

"Can Kaycee ship it to the hotel?"

"Maybe. But I'd have to order a bunch of stuff, too. That's a lot to ask the hotel to hold, and there's a good chance some of it could get lost."

"I have a better idea. You remember I played in Orlando two teams ago, right? Coach MacHolland is still there. I bet he'd be fine with you shipping stuff to his house."

"Really?"

"I'm sure of it. His wife even has one of those fancy machines that make those sticker thingies like the anchor you have on your bow. She always made T-shirts for the Wags and kids when I played there."

The wives and girlfriends of the Voltage players, collectively called the Pack, made custom shirts for just about every event. I guess every team's loved ones wanted to stand out with personalized apparel.

"It would be ideal if I didn't have to ship that, and she might"—I crossed my fingers—"even have a heat press if she does shirts. Oh, wow . . . are you sure you don't mind asking?"

"Not at all. I'll call him right after lunch."

"Thanks! You're the best."

He grinned. "I love to hear you say that."

8

KINGSTON

*A*fter lunch and the sail-away party, I upgraded the data package, and we went to check into our room. It was more spacious than I'd been expecting, which was a good thing. There was a curtain between the bed and bunks and a split bath with two separate compartments for the shower-tub and toilet, so we'd have plenty of privacy from each other.

If we wanted it.

Where had *that* thought come from? Of course we would want—and need—privacy. I reached up to pull the top bunk down from the ceiling. It looked sturdy enough to hold me, unlike most of the bigger guys on my team. I didn't weigh anywhere close to the two hundred fifty pound weight limit.

"You're not going to sleep on the sofa?" Taylor asked as she hung clothes in the closet.

"Nah. If I'm up there, we can use the sofa." I patted the bunk. "This should hold me."

"If it doesn't, I'll apologize now for laughing when it crashes down with you in it." She grinned.

"Thanks for the vote of confidence." I laid my suitcase on the armchair and unzipped it. "What are we supposed to wear to dinner?"

"Anything you want. I'm wearing this." She held up a short, royal-blue swingy dress.

A primitive, protective instinct took over my brain. "It looks short."

"It *is* short," she huffed. "When we booked this, Chels and I were both single. I'm still single, and I want to have fun, meet people, dance. Maybe even find someone who I, you know, connect with," she said with a shrug of one shoulder, avoiding my gaze.

The protector feeling kicked into higher gear. "Well, *any* single guy is going to want to connect with you wearing that. Maybe bring a sweater? Or pants. Definitely pants."

She laughed. "Are you worried about me, Brewer?"

"I promised Nate I'd look out for you. I'm a little afraid of him, so help me out a little with this?" I meant it as a joke, but my words sounded flat.

"What about you? Don't you want to . . . meet someone . . . on this vacation?" There was a waver of hesitation in her voice, and I picked up what she wasn't saying. Did she really think I'd be looking to hook up when I was here to spend time with her?

"No, I have no plans to *meet someone.* I'm here for *you* this week."

"Oh." She looked surprised. "I know that, but I thought— never mind." She shook her head and went into the shower room. I chose a blue button-down similar to the shade of her dress, black dress pants, and a tie in team colors. Maybe if we looked like we were together, single guys would steer clear.

WE TOOK THE LONG ROUTE TO DINNER, WALKING SIDE BY SIDE, our hands grazing each other's every now and again. I had to consciously resist grabbing hold. Taylor wore her hair styled down, and I wanted to run my fingers through her waterfall of waves. As her dress swirled around her shapely thighs, I prepared to glare at any guy who was gutsy enough to check her out. I fought the urge to catch her hand and lace our fingers together or put my hand on the small of her back, something, anything, to keep other guys away. I itched to touch her, even though I didn't have any right to.

A server led us to a round table where two other couples were seated and pulled out an empty chair for Taylor. I sat to her left, next to a woman about my age with long, dark hair.

I offered the woman my hand. "Hi. I'm Kingston. This is Taylor." I nodded to her, but my bubbly roommate was already absorbed in conversation with the man next to her. His accent sounded Scottish.

"Shelby." She shook my hand and gestured to the man beside her. "This is my husband, Damon, and our friends Leda and Drake."

"Great to meet you," Damon drawled. "Where are y'all from?"

"Just outside Colorado Springs. You?"

Shelby snorted. "You can't tell by his drawl? I'm kidding. We live in Maine, but this charmer is from Atlanta."

"Colorado, huh?" Leda asked, tucking her short red hair behind her ears. "I lived there for several years. I miss the skiing."

"The what?" Drake asked her.

Leda shot him a look, and he pressed his lips together. "Do you ski, Kingston?" she asked.

Taylor answered for me. "He tries. He's much better on skates, though."

"Oh really?" Shelby asked. "I love to skate. Do you skate indoors or outdoors?"

"Both," I said. "I don't get outside as often as I'd like."

"I hear that," Damon said. "My basketball hoop hardly sees me these days."

"There's a rink on the ship, right?" Shelby asked. "We should check it out. I want to see Drake on blades."

Drake paled under his trim beard. "Erm, perhaps another place—or time?"

We laughed at his less-than-enthusiastic response and settled into a lively conversation, getting to know our table-mates. Taylor told them about the Voltage, and she seemed surprised when only Leda had heard of the team. I wasn't— minor league teams are largely unknown unless you live in a city where they play.

"There's a comedy show starting in half an hour," Shelby said to me when the desserts had been cleared. "Would you and Taylor like to join us?"

"Let me check." I looked at Taylor. This weekend was all about her. I knew she had a schedule planned out.

"Yes." Taylor leaned around me to answer. "It's on the schedule. I mean, if you want to?" Her eyes searched mine as she settled back into her chair.

"Sounds good to me."

After the show, we joined our new friends in one of the lounges. Shelby sipped water while the rest of us tried the day's themed drink, the Dreamer Daiquiri. Drake and Damon seemed like great guys; older than me but young at heart. They wanted to hear about my career, and Damon shared his experiences playing college basketball.

"Hey, Brewer!" I turned to find Taylor holding two shot glasses high in the air. "It's my birthday week!" She lowered her arm and passed one to me.

Leda passed shot glasses to Drake and Damon. "Cheers to your birthday week, Taylor. May the rest of us remember how fun twenty-three was and be glad we're past it. *Salud!*"

"*Salud!*"

I tossed back the shot and moved closer to Taylor. She wrapped her arm around my waist and grinned wide. "I'm glad you're here, Brewer. Wanna do another one?" The heat from her arm was warm through my light cotton shirt, but it felt hot enough to brand me. I was cool with that. If Taylor Ranford thought I was special, I was the luckiest guy on the ship.

I'd never seen her tipsy before or as outgoing as she'd been since her wine at dinner. I did a quick mental count of how many drinks we'd had since the rum runners at lunch. At least four.

I shook my head. "Nah. How about a pair of waters?"

She pulled her lips in and scrunched her brow. "Yeah. I've probably had enough for today. Okay."

"And maybe a stroll on deck? You don't want to miss the night sky out here." I wasn't worried about her needing air as much as me needing it. The light touch of her casual side-hug still burned me from the inside out. A little ocean breeze might cool me off, but more than that, I wanted to spend time alone with her.

"That sounds nice." Damon took Shelby's hand. "What do you say, honeybee?"

"I say let's go back to our room and watch the sky from our private balcony."

"Brilliant suggestion!" Drake bent his arm, formal style, for Leda, who placed her forearm on it. He saluted us. "Till the morrow, crew."

Taylor giggled. "Does he always talk like that?"

Shelby rolled her eyes. "He does. We'll see you at breakfast?"

"See you then," I said. We watched them leave, and I went to the bar for bottled waters before we headed for the elevator bank.

"Kingston?" Taylor's hand closed around mine as we waited for the elevator.

"Yeah?" The simple touch shot straight through me, and my reaction surprised me. We'd held hands before, but this felt different somehow. The last couple of days, I hadn't been able to keep my thoughts in the friend zone. In the past, she was a buddy, a friend, but now I was reacting to her as a woman I was attracted to. The air felt charged around us, I thought about her nonstop, and I wanted to touch her, hold her hand, hug her all the time. I didn't know what to do with these new feelings. I swallowed, willing every nerve in my body to stay even and controlled.

"Is it okay if I take a rain check on the deck stroll? I'm more tired than I thought. It just hit me."

"Of course." I hoped I didn't sound disappointed.

"Cool." We stepped into the elevator, and she pressed the button for our floor. "I'm glad we have a balcony. Would you mind if we left the door open so I can fall asleep to the waves?"

"Nah. That sounds nice."

"Good." She rested the side of her head on my arm, and I dropped my chin to rest on her hair. It smelled like an orange grove.

When the door opened, I let go of her hand and wrapped my arm around her shoulders. She leaned into me as we walked to our room.

It felt nice. More than nice. Easy. Natural.

An hour later, I lay on my stomach watching her sleep, debating on closing the curtain. My heart was doing funny things, and it scared me a little.

TAYLOR

After a fun breakfast with our new friends, Kingston and I headed to the pool. I wanted to get some natural color so I wouldn't have to get a spray tan for the competition. I shuddered, thinking about the tanning salon's lemon-lime fizzy spray that tickled the inside of my nose and made me cough.

I pulled my sundress over my head and slung it over the back of the lounge chair. While Kingston took his shirt off, I put my hair up in a messy bun and set to work with my bottle of SPF 15, concentrating on the task and trying not to stare at his incredibly toned arms, pecs, and abs.

What was it about his physique that made my stomach flutter? I'd been around athletes my whole life; sculpted bodies didn't faze me or impress me. Nate was built like an Austrian bodybuilder. So what made Kingston different?

I was contemplating that question when I realized he was talking. "Hm?" I asked, bending my arm behind me to try to get every spot.

"I asked if you wanted help? I'll do you and you can do me?"

I stared at him and felt my cheeks burn. "Um, what?"

"Here." Chuckling, he stuck his hand out. I handed him the bottle and sat on the chair with my back to him.

The second his hand touched my skin, I shivered. I'd like to blame it on the lotion, but that would be a lie. His hands were gentle as he massaged the lotion slowly onto my back and shoulders. My breath caught. I definitely forgot to exhale.

Wordlessly, I returned the favor. In all the years I'd known him, I'd never touched him like this. It was such an innocent act, applying sunscreen to his back, but oh my, what a back it was.

I finished rubbing it in without completely losing my cool, and we settled into our chairs. Kingston pulled out his sketchbook, and I was reminded of the bow I needed to design. I reached into my bag for my tablet and stylus.

Glitter ribbon on metallic vinyl or metallic ribbon on glitter vinyl? And where to put the image? I drew the outline of the bow, dotted the interior to symbolize glitter, and shaded a thick band in the center of the ribbon from end to end. On one of the tails, I sketched the gym's logo. What else? I stared at it until a shadow fell over me. I looked up. Kingston cleared his throat, and his big hand closed over mine, zinging thrilling little shocks up my arm.

"Try this?" He guided my hand over the glitter vinyl sketch, adding an additional layer ribbon, a skinny, solid color that gave the design more depth.

"That's it!" I beamed up at him. "Star athlete, artist, and cheer-bow designer extraordinaire—is there anything you can't do?"

He grinned back. "Just happy to help."

"It's perfect. Thank you."

He went back to his chair and I popped in my earbuds, needing the distraction of my audiobook to clear my head.

I tried and failed to not sneak glances at Kingston. Every time I failed, he caught me and grinned, which made me smile right back. I felt a little better knowing he could feel my eyes on him, like I could his on me. It was weird but also comforting. Smiles are contagious, right? That's all this was, right?

Right?

My timer went off after sixty minutes, and I flipped over. I turned my head away from Kingston and tried to pay better attention to my audiobook.

The audio must have lulled me to sleep. "Taylor." In my dream, Kingston was whispering in my ear. "Hey, are you asleep?"

Of course I was asleep. Where else but in my dreams would Kingston be whispering in my ear?

"Poor thing must be exhausted." A woman's voice, vaguely familiar. *Get out of my dream, lady!*

"Ah, let the lass rest. Ye can let us know at dinner."

I knew *that* voice. Drake's Scottish accent was unmistakable. I lifted my head and squinted up. Where were they?

"Over here, Lorikeet." Ugh. This definitely wasn't a dream. Kingston would never call me Lorikeet in a dream. Leda and Drake stood at the foot of our chairs.

"Ay, that's a sweet endearment. She does have the voice of a songbird, does she not?"

"She does *not*." I pulled myself up and shot Kingston a look. "What's going on tonight?"

"There's a couples' game-show event." Leda grinned, her

eyes sparkling with mischief. "We're going to make sure Shelby and Damon get chosen. It's bound to be hilarious."

"Sounds fun." I pulled my legs in and crossed them. "You wanna go? It's on the schedule."

"Sure."

"Great!" Leda adjusted her wide-brimmed hat. "We'll see you at dinner!"

THE PREMISE OF PARTNER PASSION OR PERIL WAS TO SEE HOW well couples knew each other. True to her word, Leda made sure Shelby and Damon were chosen to participate.

I sat back into the round booth between Kingston and Leda. The host interviewed Shelby and Damon, who were sitting in the middle of three love seats on the stage.

"All right, folks, that's two couples. Who will be our third?" The host, a snazzily dressed guy named Chandler, turned to Shelby. "How about your friends?" He pointed to Leda and Drake, who were fidgeting and looking away in every attempt to avoid eye contact. It was more than obvious they didn't want to be chosen.

I looked around the room and giggled. Everyone had their heads down, trying to avoid eye contact. Smart.

"Hey, Chandler," Shelby called to the host, motioning with her hands for the host to come to her.

Chandler held the microphone behind his back and bent down. As Shelby spoke, a grin formed on his face. His head turned until his eyes settled on our booth. "Well, Shelby, I think that's a great idea." He stood up and put the mic to his mouth, looking directly at us. "Kingston and Taylor, you've been challenged. Come on up!"

"What?" I clutched Kingston's arm. He looked at me with an expression I couldn't read.

"Could be fun," he whispered.

"But we're not a couple," I stammered.

He winked, and my heart flipped. "Which is why it'll be fun to have bragging rights when we win this thing—and there's a money prize. Could help with grad-school expenses."

I looked back at Chandler. I could definitely use the money. It felt like everyone was staring at us.

"Everyone is staring at us," Kingston said. "What do you say?"

"Okay."

He slid out of the booth and offered his hand to pull me up. I clutched it with no intention of letting go. I didn't mind performing in front of thousands with a team, but this, being on display, rattled me.

The audience clapped as we made our way to the stage and settled on the third love seat. Kingston gave me a reassuring squeeze and rested our entwined hands on his thigh. His very muscular thigh. It felt like a rock through the denim of his jeans. I fought back a blush and gave what I hoped was a confident grin to the audience.

"So, Taylor"—Chandler stood next to me, close enough that I could smell his aftershave—"tell us how long you and Kingston have been together."

I swallowed and spoke into the mic. "Actually, we're just friends."

The host contorted his face into a dramatic frown. "I see. But you're holding hands, so that makes me wonder how close of friends you *really* are." He waggled his eyebrows smarmily at the audience.

"Not what you're thinking, man," Kingston said defensively, his eyes slitting into a warning look. "We've known each other a long time. She's one of my best friends."

"If you say so," he conceded with a skeptical frown. "Tell us where you're from and what you do and then we'll get started."

The next half hour passed in a blur. First, the guys left the room so we could answer questions about them. I think I answered most of mine right. Then we left so they could answer questions about us. When we were offstage, Shelby pulled me aside.

"You know, you two seem really good together. You sure there's nothing there?"

I pulled my lips into my mouth while I thought about how to answer. "I don't know. We are great friends. And he's ruined every guy for me since I was eleven. No one matches up to him."

"That's because no one is meant to," Sandy, the third contestant, said. "Mark my words, you two are made for each other."

"How do you know?" I asked.

"He looks at you the way my Henry looks at me." She grinned. "Just keep spending time together. I don't think it'll be long before the magic happens."

Before I could reply, Chandler opened the door to the green room. "Time to go, ladies. And good luck!"

10

KINGSTON

"If your partner could only bring one thing besides you to a desert island, what would it be?"

We were just getting started on the last round, but I was over this game. The host was especially annoying with his exaggerated facial expressions and trying-too-hard announcer voice.

After Henry and Damon answered, the question came to me. I tried to think of what Taylor would have said. "A hockey stick."

"That's correct. All three of you matched on this one. Well done!" The audience applauded. "Gentlemen, next question is about your ladies. What is her favorite book?"

I tuned out as the others answered, hoping I'd gotten it right. *"Emma,"* I said, recalling a conversation between Taylor and her sister where Chelsea argued that the movie *Clueless* was better than the original Regency-era novel. I don't know why it stuck with me, but I didn't have any other guesses.

"That's correct!"

"How did you *know* that?" Taylor's grin lit up her whole face.

I kissed her temple, and her eyes widened. Oops. "I pay attention, I guess." I quickly turned back toward the audience.

"Good work, couples! Ladies, what is your partner's favorite movie?"

"When Henry Met Sandy!" Sandy snorted as Henry lifted up his posterboard with the correct answer. "We call it that because it makes us laugh!"

The audience tittered, and Chandler gestured for Shelby to reveal her answer. *"Bad Boys Two."*

It was a match, and then it was my turn. I knew Taylor knew this one.

"D2: The Mighty Ducks." I raised my card, and she lifted her hand for a high five.

"Well done, couples. Gentlemen, which of your partner's bad habits do you dislike the most?"

Taylor didn't have any bad habits that annoyed me, but I did used to razz her about one thing. "Biting her nails?"

"Correct!" I high-fived her, remembering the first Christmas I was home from prep school. Taylor was in eighth grade, if I was doing my math right. She'd chewed her nails down to the quick, and I'd offered to paint them for her. I'd done a terrible job, and Chelsea spent a good amount of time removing the red glittery polish from Taylor's fingers afterward.

The game went on, and I couldn't help fidgeting. Taylor laid her hand on my knee, and the simple gesture of steady compassion radiated a warmth that caught me off guard. The blast was incendiary, lighting up my nerves, making my brain fuzzy, and causing me to swallow and concentrate every effort on remaining focused.

Finally, Chandler announced the last question. Oddly enough, Taylor and I were tied for first place with Henry and Sandy. Shelby and Damon were two points behind, having incorrectly guessed each other's secret talent and least favorite thing to eat. You'd think a married couple would know those things.

"What is your partner's most prized possession?"

Easy. Taylor kept hers in her parents' safe and rarely took them out. I answered quickly and confidently. "Her three college-championship rings."

Chandler frowned as the audience went quiet, and I glanced at Taylor. Her cheeks were red, and she avoided my gaze. That wasn't a good sign.

"I'm sorry, but the correct answer is a hockey puck signed by Bobby Orr. Sandy and Henry, you win!"

The Bobby Orr hockey puck was her most prized possession?

Holy hell.

Everything blurred around me as I remembered that day. That *trip.* A few years ago, I'd won four tickets, with flights and accommodations included, to the NHL's Winter Classic. Instead of taking friends from my team at the time, I asked my brother if he wanted to go. Our parents were traveling, so he suggested bringing Chelsea, and we'd needed a fourth.

It felt right for Taylor to come with us. At that point, before Jackson and Chelsea broke up, we were like family. Somehow, my coach got us souvenir pucks and VIP passes. I got to meet my favorite player, the great Bobby Orr, and he'd signed all our pucks.

That trip must have meant a hell of a lot to Taylor if her souvenir from it was her most prized possession.

I couldn't help the unsettled feeling that I was in trouble somehow.

Big trouble.

11

TAYLOR

*W*ell, that had been slightly mortifying. As Sandy and Henry celebrated their win, Chandler handed Kingston a certificate for a complimentary couple's massage. I smiled sheepishly at him. His surprise at my answer threw me off guard. That trip had been a marker event in our friendship, at least for me. We'd partnered up for everything, and I hadn't felt like the "best friend's little sister" anymore. I'd felt like we were really, truly friends after that point.

We said goodnight to our tablemates and headed back to our cabin. Kingston had that in-the-zone face that he got when he was trying to work something out in his head, so I hadn't wanted to say anything to interrupt his thoughts.

When we reached the room, he unlocked the door and gestured for me to go in first. I went straight to the glass door and stepped out onto the balcony, turning my face into the wind. I felt him next to me as my hair blew wildly.

"Taylor?"

I turned my head, and my hair whipped around my face. I did my best to tuck as much of it as I could behind my ears.

"Not your rings?"

"No." I tried to keep my face neutral to hide the bile that burned my throat every time I thought about that one championship we lost my freshman year. The one that had broken the school's twenty-year winning streak. "They remind me of the one I don't have. The year we lost Nya."

"Your teammate who—*oh*." He gave me a side-hug, and I leaned my head against him.

"Yeah," I whispered. Nya had fallen from a stunt, and we'd lost. She'd gotten back up to finish the routine, but the damage had been done—to our score and her spine. She forced herself to finish the routine and injured herself worse after landing the last basket toss sideways in the cradle. She hadn't been able to live with the failure or the news that she could never cheer again. The surgery she needed was risky and could cause paralysis. All she'd ever done her whole life was cheer; she didn't know anything else, didn't want to *be* anything else.

After Nya took her life, I changed my major from exercise physiology to sports psychology. Athletes of all ages were under a lot of pressure, and I learned I had a gift for helping them navigate it. I also wanted to help retired athletes find a path after they couldn't play anymore.

"Why did you say the puck?" His blue eyes blazed with sincerity as they connected with mine. He pulled away from me and rested his forearms on the railing.

I shrugged. "It was an unforgettable trip."

"It was. For me. I guess I didn't think it mattered to you."

I leaned on the rail next to him, my elbow just inches from his. I decided to be honest. "It mattered a lot."

"Why?"

How could I say this without revealing how I felt? Without admitting to my decade-plus crush on him?

I couldn't. I phrased my answer carefully. "It was exciting being with you, in your element. And we became good friends on that trip."

He held my gaze and spoke in a low, rumbly tone. "Is that what we are? Good friends?"

I pressed my lips together and searched his face for a sign, wondering if there were lines to read between in his question.

"I hope so," I whispered. "Even better friends, since you came back." I held my breath and willed him to respond or break eye contact, anything. My heart pounded in my chest.

"We are, definitely." He stood up, and without thinking, I mirrored his movement and looked up into the face I needed to see every day, wanted to touch, and kiss, and—

I gasped when his hand grazed my chin. He immediately pulled it down to his side. *No, no, no, no, no! Touch the chin! Lean in! Kiss me already!*

I wanted to scream, but of course, I didn't. I just stood there, frozen, unable to speak.

Kingston swallowed and nodded toward the door. "Wanna watch a movie?"

My shoulders sagged. I tried to keep my chin up, but I failed. I wanted so much more from him, even if I was terrified to admit it. If he didn't reciprocate, I'd be crushed. Being stuck in the cabin with him for a few days after being rejected paled in comparison to the thought of seeing him regularly for the rest of my life, wanting him, and knowing he hadn't wanted me back.

"Let me just change into pajamas first," I blurted. Before he could answer, I was through the door.

HOURS LATER, THE SHIP'S HORN PULLED ME FROM A DREAMLESS sleep. My neck hurt, and I didn't want to face the light I felt on my eyelids.

It didn't take me long to realize I wasn't in my bed. Neither was Kingston.

He was behind me, spooning me, on the sofa. I had to still be dreaming.

Nope. I could feel his heart beating into my back.

His left arm held my waist tightly. His even breathing signaled he was still asleep, which left me with two options. Wake him up, or don't?

For selfish reasons, I decided to pretend to still be asleep. I didn't want to disturb him, but even more than that, I wanted to bask in every second he held me in his arms. I felt safe, cared for, important, and I wanted every moment of it that he was willing to give—even if he didn't know it.

The ship's horn blew again. The boat rocked gently, and I assumed we were docking. I was not about to open my eyes to confirm that, though.

His chin rubbed at my messy bun. "Heeeeeeey."

I didn't move.

The rumble of Kingston's groggy whisper was a command to my goosebumps to wake up. I pressed my eyes shut and hoped he wouldn't notice. *One more minute, just one more minute.*

He shifted behind me and cleared his throat. "Taylor? You awake?"

Nope. Not awake. Still sleeping.

I felt him trying to maneuver his body around me, so I opened my eyes guiltily. "Hey." I pulled my knees to my chest so he could scoot around me and off the sofa.

"Thanks." He kissed the top of my head. All these little displays of affection were really starting to mess with my head. "I'll be right back."

I sat up slowly and looked outside. Our ship was docked, parked next to a massive vessel that dwarfed ours. Even in its shade, the sunlight was bright enough to sting my eyes.

The toilet flushed, bringing me out of my fantasy. Nothing like real life to jerk you back to reality. I closed my eyes again, trying to imagine away the *whoosh* of the flush and stream of the faucet so I could return to my fantasy.

My eyes snapped open at the squeak of the toilet closet's door. Kingston returned wearing striped board shorts and a navy rash guard that fit him like second skin. His Brewski's ball cap sat backward on his head, the restaurant's logo just above his forehead, atop his perfect face, which was dusted with overnight stubble. He sat on my bed. "Mornin'. You sleep okay?"

Why did that sound awkward?

I forced a grin. "Yes, thanks. How . . .?" I gestured to the sofa.

He swallowed, lifted his cap, and ran his fingers through his hair. "We were sitting up, and you fell asleep on my shoulder. I guess at some point we fell over and adjusted?"

I willed myself not to blush. "Makes sense."

"So . . . snorkeling?"

"Yes, I've never been. You?"

"A few times. You'll love it."

"Can't wait." And if I hated it, I'd still be in the ocean, with Kingston, on a beautiful sunny day in paradise.

12

KINGSTON

*S*norkeling with Taylor was like watching a kid open gifts at Christmas. Everything delighted her, and she kept forgetting that smiling allowed water to leak into her mouthpiece. We had to surface at least a handful of times for her to spit out water and adjust her tube. By the third time, it became a schtick, and my abs hurt from laughing at and with her.

When we finished, we were sandy, salty, and high on life. She suggested shopping for outfits for the decades party that night. I followed her around the brightly painted island shops like an excited puppy. I'd wear anything she asked me to.

By the time we sat down for lunch at an outdoor cafe, we'd visited a least a dozen stores, but we hadn't purchased anything. I pulled the brim of my ball cap lower on my forehead to shade me from the sun's glare as we were seated. Taylor's cheeks and shoulders were rosy, and tendrils of her sandy hair framed her face. The pink hue enhanced her beauty, and I couldn't help smiling. She sighed with contentment as she settled into the seat across from me.

"So," I said. "Have you decided what we're wearing?"

"Maybe." She pressed her lips together. "Your suggestion about the nineties has grown on me. I've always wanted to dress up like Britney Spears in that schoolgirl outfit, but I've never had the guts to."

"You could totally pull that off, Lorikeet." Her cheeks pinkened deeper, and my slow grin widened.

She blew out a breath but didn't comment on the usage of the nickname this time. "Mm-hmm." She regarded me wryly. "You don't think that short skirt would attract attention?"

I grinned. "Guaranteed. But I'll fight them off for you. Plus, your cheer skirts are shorter than that plaid skirt you were looking at."

She laughed. "Speaking of plaid . . ."

"Yeah?"

"You can go grungy. I know you want to. It's an easy outfit. Wear your jeans and a T-shirt, and we can get you a flannel. Easy peasy, and we'll look coordinated for the event's souvenir picture."

I toyed with my napkin, trying to keep my expression cool as it sunk in that it was important to her how we looked for the event photo. Yesterday, I'd been the one who wanted to coordinate, though I hadn't vocalized it. I wanted people to know that she was with me, that we were together. Not *together*, but together . . . Was I reading too much into her words?

After lunch, we returned to the shop to buy the plaids and reboarded the ship. On the desk in the cabin, the certificate for the complimentary couple's massage caught my eye.

"When do you want to . . ." I nodded toward the paper.

She followed my gaze. "I could use that now, actually. Do you think they take walk-ins?"

"If they have openings, no doubt. Want me to call?"

"I'll do it." She picked up the cabin's phone and dialed the spa. As I waited, images of a towel-clad Taylor danced in my head. I hadn't thought until now about disrobing.

She covered the receiver. "They have an opening in forty-five minutes. Can we make that? It'll leave us plenty of time to get ready for the party tonight. Otherwise, they can fit us in tomorrow morning."

"Right now works for me." She gave me a thumbs-up and turned away to set the appointment with the spa receptionist.

When she hung up the phone, she stared at it, brow creased and lips pressed together. "So are people usually naked for these things?"

I laughed and sat on the bed. "Usually. You need your back clear." I regarded her with interest. "Haven't you gotten massages before?"

"Yes, but always by myself and always with a woman. Our appointment is with Gustav and Viggo."

I burst out laughing, unable to control the delight at seeing her so adorably perplexed. She shot me a glare, then started laughing herself. I pulled her to sit next to me on the bed and gave her a reassuring side-hug. "Maybe stay in your underwear then?"

She sighed, resting her head on my shoulder. "Hmm . . . I think I'll wear my strapless bathing suit and just undo it when I need to. What do you think?"

I had a lot of thoughts about that but none I would speak out loud. "Sounds like a plan." When she got up to go change, I went to the fridge for a cold water. I pressed the bottle to my forehead. The AC was as high as it could go, but I was suddenly very hot.

13

TAYLOR

*T*he couple's massage presented a lot of details I hadn't anticipated. Had I thought it out, I probably would've suggested giving it to Damon and Shelby.

We arrived at the spa and were handed electronic tablets to complete a series of health-related questions and then were ushered into a small changing room. Together.

I watched Kingston pull off his shirt and slip out of his slides. He pulled at the cord on his swim trunks, and I heard myself gasp. His hand stilled, and he looked up at me.

"Give me a chance to at least turn around before you"—I gestured wildly—"before you *disrobe.*" I couldn't bring myself to say "get naked" out loud.

He grinned wickedly, but then concern fell over his features. "I can keep this on if you'd feel more comfortable."

"Yes!" I shouted. One of his eyebrows raised. "Sorry, I didn't mean to shout. Okay. Let's do this." I pulled my coverup over my head and reached for my robe. We'd been swimming together a lot in the time we'd known each other. I'd done this more times than I could count over the last ten-plus years, and yet, in here, today, it felt different. More intimate. Crazy intimate.

From the serious expression on his face, he felt something, too. A shift. Subtle. But definitely noticeable. Kingston looked away and slid his arms into the sleeves of the lush white terrycloth robe. I took a deep breath and tied the belt of my mine securely at my waist.

He opened the curtain, and I followed him out. The attendant was waiting and led us to a nearby room. Gentle, calming music played, and soft lighting illuminated two freshly made-up tables. "Gustav and Viggo will be in shortly. Wait under the sheets, facedown."

The door closed, and we hung up our robes in silence. I stared at the padded, sheet-clad tables but made no move toward them. Kingston took my hand, giving it a reassuring squeeze, and towed me to the space in the center of them. Wordlessly, he pulled back the top sheet on the table closest to him and climbed in. As promised, he left his shorts on.

I mimicked his actions at the other table and placed my face in the donut-shaped pad that extended from the table. My face was burning, betraying my efforts to be calm and cool. I wondered if he'd noticed it in the dim light.

A moment later, the massage therapists entered, and I concentrated on clearing my mind and just being in the moment. Mercifully, I was able to finally relax. Halfway through, I groggily turned over and lost myself in Viggo's giant hands as he worked at the muscles in my neck and head.

Too soon, it was over. Viggo stretched my right arm straight out, and I found my fingers in Kingston's sturdy grip. The therapists left the room, and we lay there in silence, neither one of us wanting to break the connection.

14

KINGSTON

I wasn't sure how much time had passed, but the knock on the door jolted me out of my dazed contentment. Throughout the massage, all I could think about was Taylor, next to me, and Viggo's hands kneading her tired muscles in places I craved to touch and bring comfort to. At times, her breathing changed, and I wondered if she was experiencing relief or pain. Every little gasp and sigh had me reacting in ways that were definitely not the friend-zone type.

We walked back to the room in silence. I wondered if she'd been affected similarly. We kept looking at each other on the walk, and each time our eyes met, Taylor blushed and looked away.

It was driving me wild.

I keyed open the door and yanked open the drawer that held my athletic shorts and T-shirts. "I'm gonna go for a run."

"I'll shower and get ready while you're out. Dinner is early tonight, remember."

"I won't be gone long." I changed quickly, grabbed a bottle of water, and broke into a sprint as soon as I hit the hallway. I ran up the stairs to the lido deck, where a running path snaked around the perimeter of the ship. Around the adult quiet pool, then the rock-climbing wall, ice rink, and shuffleboard courts.

I slowed to a stop at the basketball hoops, where a familiar figure dribbled, darted, and spun on the court. Damon slam-dunked the ball into the net, caught it on the rebound, and dribbled it out to the foul line. He tossed it toward the net and jogged to the hoop to catch it after it swished through. Up again for a layout, catching it again before he noticed me watching through the chain-link barrier.

"Stop staring and come around," he called, tucking the ball under one arm. He wiped his forehead on the end of his loose black athletic tank and nodded to the door in the fence. "You shoot hoops?"

"Not like you. But give me a stick and a puck . . ."

He shook his head and laughed. "Don't let Shelby hear you say that. She'll roll her eyes so far into the back of her head, they'll disappear."

"Women," we said at the same time.

He tossed me the ball. "First to eleven?"

"Let's do it."

I held my own pretty well, but I was no match for his fancy moves or speed. I lost by two and earned a fist bump and nod of appreciation.

"Good game." Damon checked his watch. "My time's up in five." He carried the ball over to the bench where we'd left our waters. He downed a full bottle. "You wanna go again?"

"Nah." I sipped from mine. "I blew off the steam I needed. Thanks."

"Steam, huh? Everything okay with you and Taylor?" We

straddled the ends of the bench, facing each other but looking out toward the water. The ship cut through the waves, the light breeze soothing my damp skin.

"We did that couple's massage, and I needed to burn off some . . . energy."

He snorted. "Yeah, I get that. You gonna make a move or what?"

I looked at him, surprised. "You think I should? What if it doesn't work out?"

"What if it does? Imagine how different the next few days will be. The summer, the future. Do you see her in it long-term?"

I turned back to the ocean. "I'd like to. But we have different dreams." I filled him in on her plans and my contract issues. "Did you have dreams of playing in the NBA?"

"What kid doesn't dream of playing at the top level some-day?" He lifted the ball and twirled it on his finger. I watched it spin. "By the end of college, though, I just wanted to get out into the world and make a difference in my community. Help the kids get the chance I had."

"I didn't go to college," I confessed. "The only other skill I have is the ability to draw comic figures."

"Did you ever think about pursuing an art degree? You could do that in the summers."

I shrugged. "I took a few classes virtually when I was younger. General stuff. But school was always hard for me."

"Don't underestimate yourself. You're older now. You've learned a lot and lived a lot since then. You can always go back, unless you want to coach?"

I shrugged. "Maybe. I just wanna play as long as I can."

"I get that. And when you're done, you'll know you're

done, without a doubt." We stood as a pair of teens entered the court.

I lifted my hand for a fist bump, and he wrapped his arm around me for a quick man-hug. "Thanks for the game."

He grinned. "Anytime. See you at dinner."

Taylor was in the shower room when I got back. I was sitting out on the balcony with my sketchpad when she called out to let me know it was my turn to get ready.

I stopped short at the threshold. I think I blinked a few times. A warmness filled me as I took her in. She stood in front of the mirror, parting her hair down the middle with the tail of a long comb. Her long-sleeved white shirt was unbuttoned to the waist and tied in a knot, revealing a low-cut black tank top underneath. The pleated skirt fell just below the curve of her backside, and her sculpted legs were on full display. She completed the look with no-show socks and her white cheer sneakers.

I stared at her shoes because I didn't want to get busted staring anywhere else.

"It was either the cheer shoes or flip-flops. My black heels are too fancy."

"Hm? Oh. Yeah. You'll be more comfortable in those, right?"

"Yeah, but I'm so *short* in these." She sighed as she pulled a section of hair into a covered elastic and pulled it tight to her head. "I was thinking about asking Leda if she might have something I could borrow. She's about my size."

I stood directly behind her, and our eyes met in the mirror. I laid my hands lightly on her shoulders. Her one ponytail tickled my neck. I could rest my chin on her head, but I didn't. I wanted to say size didn't matter, that she was perfect the way she was. Instead, I tried to make a joke. "Haven't you heard that good things come in small packages?"

Taylor snorted, and I wrapped my arms around her, bending down so that our faces were next to each other. We stared at our reflection for just a little too long. I gotta admit, I really liked the picture I saw.

She leaned into me, tilted her head, and spoke to our reflections in a low voice. "That is so cliché, Brewer, but if you say so . . ."

I chuckled and shook my head at her implication. "That's what I hear," I clarified, shrugging as I pulled away from her with a grin. I needed to get to that shower and remind myself about the friend-zone rules.

15

TAYLOR

*O*ur tablemates were *fun*.

Dinner was lively, and conversation mostly revolved around our costume choices. Drake and Leda were dressed as flower children in leather fringe vests. She wore a waist-length black wig, hiding her auburn hair, and a short yellow minidress with go-go boots. Shelby and Damon, dressed as preppy versions of Sandy and Danny from *Grease*, looked straight out of a fifties diner. We had a blast posing for a group picture outside the entrance to the event.

The decades party was in full swing when the six of us arrived, and Kingston pulled me straight onto the dance floor so I wouldn't miss rocking out to one of my favorite boy-band songs. He used to tease me about my obsession with One Direction, but all was forgiven as he sang along to the lyrics. I pretended he meant it as he belted out the part about lighting up his world like nobody else.

If only.

Harry Styles's voice faded into a synthesized eighties dance song. Shelby, Damon, and Leda joined us, and we formed a small circle. I looked for Drake and spotted him leaning against the bar, eyes bright and lips twitching as he watched us. He held a small glass of what I presumed was rum after he'd made a point to tell us at dinner how he planned to try every variety of the spirit that the ship offered.

I turned when someone tapped my left shoulder. A tall man with colored sunglasses and a mop of bleach-blond curls, dressed from head to toe in baggy denim, grinned at me. I exchanged a glance with Leda and stifled a laugh when she waggled her eyebrows. I politely declined the not-very-look-alike Justin Timberlake's offer for a dance and turned back to my group, where I was immediately swooped into Kingston's arms as the music changed again.

"Scuse me!" Leda shouted. "Drake's not sitting out this one!"

"(I've Had) The Time of My Life" started off slow. I looked up at Kingston and wondered if our relationship was changing. Our eyes locked, and I had to look away. His serious expression as he softly mouthed the words took my breath away. It was an equal mix of delightful and awkward.

Over his shoulder, I almost couldn't believe what I was seeing. "Oh my gosh, look!" Drake held Leda in a perfect ball-room hold and led her effortlessly in a waltz that picked up speed in tandem with the song.

Kingston turned so we could watch them. He rested our linked hands against his heart, and I dropped my grip on his shoulder, snaking it around his waist. I was feeling the romance and love between our new friends, and it was making me all gooey inside. Everyone was backing away from the dance floor, and when the song finished, Drake and Leda took a bow and headed for the bar. I glanced up at Kingston and decided I needed a drink, too.

"I'll be right back. Girl meeting at the bar." I nodded to where Shelby and Leda were at the long wooden counter. "Can I get you a drink?"

"I'd love one. But only if I can get the next round."

"Of course. What do you want?"

His eyes flickered dark for a millisecond, then he gave a half smile. "Surprise me."

"Will do!" I squeezed his hand and felt his eyes on me as I scurried to the bar and squeezed in next to Leda. The bartender took my order right away, and I blew out a long breath, inflating my cheeks in an attempt to force myself to calm down.

"So you two really aren't together?" Leda asked before I could comment about her performance. She took a sip of wine and turned so that her back was to the counter. "That guy who asked you to dance was cute. Why say no if you're single?"

I shook my head. "I wasn't feeling it. He's not what I'm looking for."

Shelby took a sip of her water and leaned around Leda. "What exactly *are* you looking for?"

I sighed dramatically and nodded toward my ideal guy, who was standing only a few feet away. "Someone like Kingston. No one else comes close. He's ruined all men for me."

"Hmm." Leda looked past me to where the guys were standing where we'd left them. "Sounds to me you've put him on some type of pedestal. Is he deserving of it?"

"Yeah, he is." I wasn't blind to his faults and struggles, but I had a front row seat to his goodness and perseverance. I told them about how he was my sister's best friend, how he was always kind and respectful. "He's really the best kind of friend anyone could ask for. And he's been around so long, he's like family." I snapped my mouth shut as the guys approached.

Drake frowned at us. I tried not to giggle as his long hair, parted in the middle like a hippie's, kept falling in his face. "What's got you ladies so serious?"

"We're looking for a man for Taylor." Leda slid her arm across my shoulders.

"A man?" Drake's gaze darted to Kingston, whose expression was unreadable.

Shelby rolled her eyes. "You know, a person. Like a woman, but with different parts."

"Erm." His cheeks reddened, and I laughed. With another glance at Kingston, Drake pointed toward the end of the bar at a man in a zoot suit nursing a beer by himself. "That fellow looks a bit lonely."

"Too broody," Shelby said and nodded toward a trio dressed as Ghostbusters. "How 'bout one of those? Specifically, the tall one with the glasses?"

"He looks like a fine chap!" Drake agreed.

Damon nodded to Kingston. "Y'all let me know if you need help with the security for Ms. Spears. We don't want a *circus.*"

I snorted. Damon's play on Britney's hit song was funny, but it had me wondering if my outfit was a little too much. I'd noticed guys looking at me all night. Were Kingston's little acts of affection more for his benefit or mine?

The bartender set down the rum runners I'd ordered, and as I held one out to Kingston, I felt my phone vibrate. I pulled it from my waistband, noticing he, too, was fiddling with his phone. I swiped to answer when I saw it was Chelsea.

"Hey, how are you feeling, and can I call you back?" I spoke fast and loud into the phone. "We're at a party!"

"Much better, and no! You definitely cannot." She giggled hoarsely. "Are you with Kingston?"

"Yes!" I glanced at him as he swiped to answer his own call.

"Good. Jackson called him in case you were apart. I'm going to do a countdown. Ready? Three . . . two . . . one . . . we're engaged!"

"Yes!" I screamed. "Congratulations! Let me leave the party so you can tell me all about it—"

"No, no, no! You go dance, have fun, and don't worry about me. We still have a ton of people to tell. Call me tomorrow, okay?"

"Okay!" I hung up the phone and high-fived Kingston. "It's about time!" And then a thought occurred to me. "Wait. How long has he been planning this?"

"Months." Kingston grinned. "He was planning to do it in Florida. He had a ticket to fly in when the ship docked and sweep her away to a beach resort. But when she got sick, he made a new plan."

"Okay. For a second, I thought—"

"Taylor, she really was and still is sick."

"Yeah, I know. Never mind." I felt guilty the thought that my sister or future brother-in-law might have played up her illness to keep her from the cruise had even popped into my head.

"Are you going to fill us in so we can celebrate with you?" Shelby asked.

Kingston's grin widened. He looked up from his phone

and flashed the screen, a selfie of the newly engaged couple. "My brother just asked his girlfriend to marry him."

"That's wonderful!" Shelby lifted her water glass. "A toast then." She turned to me. "And the bride-to-be is your friend?"

"She's my sister."

Shelby's smile faltered for a millisecond before she yelled, "So you weren't kidding when you said you were like family. Cool. Cheers!"

16

KINGSTON

I couldn't have been happier for my brother and Chelsea. Their engagement had been a long time coming. I wanted what they had.

And I wanted it with Taylor. That became abundantly clear when Jackson shared his news, hitting me like a ninety-mile-per-hour puck to my heart. I fought between the protective affection and a newer sensation. I didn't want to name it, but I knew what it was. I didn't want her to be my sister or sister-in-law or whatever it was called when your brother marries someone who has a sister. Was it anything?

I was falling in love with her, and I couldn't stop it. I didn't *want* to stop it. I wanted to skate full speed ahead right into her heart.

Sometimes I thought she felt the same way, but then she'd pull back. It was clear she didn't want to dance with a random guy. We were good together, and we both knew it.

So what was stopping us? Our siblings' relationship? Our unspoken friend-zone rule?

Fear it wouldn't work out? That it wouldn't last if I had to leave Colorado again to play hockey?

Forget it all. I was taking my chance. A shot of adrenaline burned within as I hugged her, holding her for longer than was probably normal. I fought the urge to kiss her right there and spill my guts.

I wanted her. Hell, I *needed* her. Somehow, she'd replaced Chelsea as my best friend in the last year, and the thought of her dating, or marrying, anyone else stirred bile in my gut.

I had to do something.

Now.

I needed her to know how I felt. Maybe not the extent of it, but something. I didn't want to lose her to one of the chumps who had been ogling her all night. Or anyone else.

If you don't take the shot, you have zero chance of scoring.

My dad's voice played in my head. How many times had he told me that when I was a kid? He'd played hockey, too, and had coached me until high school.

When she shifted to let go, I tightened my arms around her. I whisper-shouted into the feathery poof at the top of one of her braided pigtails. "Come for a walk with me?"

She nodded, and I reluctantly released her. She plucked our drinks off the bar and addressed our new friends. "We're going to take a walk. See you later?"

"Later." Shelby winked at her. Hmm. I took my drink, and we said our goodbyes.

Out in the hall, I considered my options before turning left. The hall led to a dining room that was closed at this hour. Right would take us to the elevators.

"Where are we going?" Taylor's sweet voice fueled my urgency.

I pulled her around the corner, took her drink, and set our glasses on the floor. I didn't dare speak for fear of starting a conversation or chickening out. Instead, I lifted both hands to her face, using my index fingers to trace lines from her temples to the tiny cleft in her chin to the full bottom lip she nibbled lightly.

I splayed my fingers over her cheeks, and we stared into each other's eyes, neither of us daring to move. After what seemed like an eternity, she gave the slightest nod, her light eyes filled with consent and framed by long, wispy lashes. Her lips parted, and suddenly, I was nervous. I swallowed, needing a second to take it all in. I wanted this moment to be perfect.

This was it.

I was going to kiss Taylor Ranford.

I lowered my head to hers. She lifted on her toes and pressed her lips to mine. A flash of white light blinded me as I closed my eyes, and the expression "seeing stars" suddenly made sense. Taylor's lips were soft on mine, almost unsure.

I wasn't unsure.

I'd never been *more* sure of anything in my entire life.

She wrapped her arms around my neck, locking me into place in her embrace. Encouraged, I deepened our kiss. For an immeasurable amount of time, we were each other's air. Our hearts pounded against each other, and I'd never felt so close to another human being.

There was no coming back from this.

There was no coming back from this.

Our world was forever changed with one kiss. I hoped to God we could make this work and that it wouldn't be awkward at future family gatherings with Chelsea and Jackson. If either pair of us ever broke up . . .

I realized I didn't care.

Taylor sighed as she broke our kiss. I opened my eyes to find her staring at me. Her eyes glistened, and a single tear traced a path down her cheek, where it came to a halt at the side of my thumb.

I let go of her face, unable to find words as more tears followed the first. I could only watch. Why was she crying? Had I misread her?

No, that couldn't be it. She'd kissed me back with the same fervor. Then what was it?

She gave a little laugh and unlatched her hands from behind my neck, letting them come to a rest just inside my shoulders. "These are happy tears, Brewer. I've waited so long for you to kiss me."

The thumping in my heart sped up, cheered by her words. "I'm sorry it took so long, then," I whispered.

"It was worth the wait."

"Yeah?" I tipped up her chin. This was Taylor. *My* Taylor. I'd known her since she was a kid. But she hadn't been a kid for a long time, and now that I'd done it, it felt like I'd wanted to kiss her all my life.

"Is something wrong?" she asked. "Maybe I shouldn't have said that . . ."

"No, no, nothing's wrong. It's just I've dreamed about this."

Her eyes widened. "You've dreamed about this? When?"

I met her gaze and went with the truth. "Every time I saw you." I hadn't been able to admit that to myself. I'd been such a fool, not even allowing myself to consider taking our friendship to the next level.

We looked at each other, neither of us speaking. I pulled

her to me and cradled her head against my heart. "This feels so right, Taylor. Us."

"I always knew it would," she whispered.

WE NEVER MADE IT BACK TO THE PARTY. AFTER A MARATHON make-out session on our balcony, we tore ourselves away from each other and went to our separate beds. I tossed and turned in the pull-down berth, and from the sounds on the other side of the curtain, Taylor was equally restless. I wanted to fall asleep with her in my arms, but I didn't want to push her too far, too fast.

17

TAYLOR

*I*t had been hard to quiet my mind last night after all the kissing. Eventually, the waves lulled me to sleep. The ship's horn, signaling our arrival in Nassau, roused me from a satisfied slumber.

My lips still tingled with Kingston's affection. Gentle but passionate, he hadn't used a lot of words, and if his touch conveyed his true feelings, there was no doubt in my mind he felt something important between us.

I rolled over onto my back and stared at the crop of unruly hair that peeked over from the pullout berth. My eyes lingered until his phone alarm trilled, and after he silenced it, he rolled onto his stomach and lifted his head, grinning when he noticed me looking at him.

I smiled back shyly. "Good morning."

"Great morning," he corrected.

I blushed. And for once, I didn't care. *Yes. Yes, it was.* The first day of what I dared hope would be #Taylorand-Kingston4eva.

I wouldn't say that out loud though. Not yet. Maybe never.

But the inner preteen with the crush on her sister's best friend was in heaven, giddy with the realization that she'd not only finally kissed Kingston Brewer, but that he actually cared for her. That maybe he might think I was his endgame.

He slid off his bed and padded to the balcony. I followed him into the bright sunshine and wrapped my arms around his waist, pressing my cheek to his bare back. He turned around and planted a chaste kiss on my lips, and I wished I'd thought to brush my teeth before joining him outside.

"What's on the agenda today?" he asked, placing his large hands over mine. He stroked the tops of my fingers, and I tried to form thoughts to answer his question.

"You haven't skated in a few days." I glanced up at his perfect face. "You wanna hit the onboard rink?"

He shook his head. "Maybe tomorrow. Today, I want to do what you want to do."

Those words, backed by the intensity in his eyes, had me on the verge of combusting. I swallowed and tried to rein my thoughts back to the schedule from where they'd taken a turn for Kingstonville. "I'd like to go to the Pirate and Treasure Museum this morning. Especially since tonight is the pirate party. Unless you've already been to the museum on your previous cruise?"

"Nope. That sounds fun. Drake mentioned it last night. He wants to see if they've got any artifacts from a pirate called Captain Kilt."

I giggled. "Kilt, as in the skirt, or killed, the past tense of kill?"

"I didn't ask. They're heading out right after breakfast, though."

"Perfect. Let's get to breakfast, then."

Kingston's interest in pirates had surprised and delighted me, and *his* costume was driving me mad. Ruffly shirt half-unbuttoned, body-hugging leather breeches, and adorable Colonial-era buckle shoes. He wore a long black wig and a hat similar to Drake's perched on his head, but his hat was embellished with a large white ostrich plume.

Watching Drake interact with, and comment on, the exhibits at the pirate museum was a riot. He had something to say about every artifact and challenged our tour guide—politely, of course—at least a handful of times. I wondered how he knew so much about pirates, privateers, and buccaneers.

"You looked ready to draw an imaginary sword! Are you a historian?" I asked him that night at dinner. The dining room had been decorated to the night's theme, and I was happy to see our friends had gone all out on their costumes, like Kingston and I had. I loved dressing up, pretending I was someone else for a bit. It gave me confidence and made for great memories.

Drake adjusted his tricorn hat and glanced at Leda, who was hiding a smile behind her wine glass. "Erm, yes. Well, you see, Captain Kilt was not killed in St. Augustine in 1717. The Spanish did not sink his ship as they attempted their escape."

Kingston leaned forward, and his hand holding mine under the table shifted slightly, grazing my skin just above the knee, where my boots stopped. The over-the-knee leather boots had been a splurge in a moment when I'd been feeling brave. I'd never felt so desirable, and I wasn't sure how I felt about it. Just that it felt good, and I wanted him to look at me

that way as often as possible. As if I was the only thing—
person—he ever wanted or needed to look at.

"How can you know for sure?" Kingston asked Drake. "I
googled the *Santa Sofia* while you two were arguing. There's
no record of it after the siege on the fort in 1717."

"Yes, well, I can see how one might arrive at that conclu-
sion. A very valuable treasure was stolen by Kilt's crew. But
there's a sketch of the ship in a museum in Charleston, placing
it next to Blackbeard's galleon in May of 1718. That bloke at
the museum—the *expert,* as he called himself—refused to take
into consideration he might have incorrect information."

Leda put her wine down and picked up her phone. "We
visited Charleston a while back. I just remembered I have a
picture of it!"

Kingston took the phone from her, and Damon and Shelby
leaned in. "It definitely looks legit," Kingston said. "The artist
did a great job capturing the spirit and tone of the
waterfront."

"Yes, I think so," Drake agreed. "Some say Captain Kilt
sketched it himself, but I'm not sure I believe that."

Kingston nodded. "Whoever painted it, it's a brilliant use
of watercolor. It must have been hard to get it to set just right
on the parchment."

"'Tis indeed. Are you an artist, Kingston?" Drake asked.

Kingston smiled shyly. "Not really. I used to paint, but I
gave it up when I got serious about hockey. I mostly just draw
now."

"Don't be modest." I gave him a playful shove and told the
table about Adam and his superhero comic books.

"That's so nice," Damon said. I noted sadness in his eyes. "I
was a Big Brother when I lived in Atlanta. Working with kids

can teach you more than you impart on them." He'd kept his costume simple. Just a faux-leather vest over a lace-up white shirt that exposed a good amount of his toned light-brown skin. He was just as fit as Kingston, though taller and bulkier, and I once again wondered what it was about Kingston in particular that attracted me to him and not anyone else.

Shelby patted his hand and caught his gaze. "You should see him with my nephew. He's five and thinks the moon comes out for Damon." She laughed.

He flicked a smile at her and lifted his beer. "Noah's a great kid. I can't wait to give him cousins."

Shelby blushed. Leda grinned at her, as if they shared a secret, and I wondered if that was the reason Shelby was drinking water. I must have been looking at her glass, because she laughed and stated emphatically, "I'm not pregnant. Yet."

"Well, it ain't for lack of trying!" Damon quipped. She slugged him on the shoulder, and we all laughed. I snuck a glance at Kingston. I caught and returned his broad smile.

"Look at you two," Shelby observed. "All sweet and googly-eyed. You never made it back to the party last night, and after watching you together today, I think I need an insulin shot."

My salad became the most interesting thing in my line of sight. Kingston let go of my hand and pulled me close to him. I rested my head on his shoulder and hoped my flaming cheeks were subdued by my heavy foundation and eyeliner-drawn fake scars. He kissed the top of my head. "It's been a long time coming," he said.

"Well, we're happy for you." Leda raised her glass. "Cheers!"

"Cheers!"

We finished dinner and went to the main lobby, which had

been transformed to look like the main deck of a pirate ship. Kingston pulled me back onto the dance floor at arm's length, and his eyes drifted, sweeping me from head to toe. My throat caught when he trailed his fingers lightly from my ear, down the side of my neck, and over my bare shoulder, stopping when they encountered the fabric of my white shirt. I shuddered against his hard, warm torso, the thin costume fabrics not much of a barrier between us.

"What?" I whispered.

"Would it be offensive if I said you were the hottest pirate wench I'd ever seen?"

"And how many hot pirate wenches have you seen?" I pulled at one of his fake dreadlocks.

"Enough to know I don't want to see any more." He swallowed and held my gaze. For a second, I thought he might kiss me. But then he gave his head a little shake and grinned, sinking into a formal bow, his hand raised. "Care to dance, fair lady?"

I giggled. "Most certainly, Captain Brewer."

Halfway through the song, he let go of my waist and brought his hand to my cheek. "This is real, right? You, me, us?"

"Yes," I whispered. "Very real."

His soft lips met mine, catapulting my heart rate and setting every nerve to sizzling. I knew now that this kind of connection of the heart, soul, and body was real, and it just further proved my theory that Kingston had stolen my heart the first time I saw his smile when I was a kid. No one else had ever incited butterflies in me like he did. There wasn't anything about this guy that wasn't perfect for me.

18

KINGSTON

"*B*est birthday ever," Taylor murmured into my shoulder as we swayed on the dance floor. It was well after midnight, and the pirate party was winding down. She sighed contentedly, and I tightened my arms around her. All I could think about was how I wanted to hold her like this forever. I was falling hard and fast for Taylor, losing control of my emotions . . . and it felt right.

"It's not your birthday yet," I whispered, teasing her. "What time were you born again?"

"One sixteen a.m."

Leda tapped me on the shoulder. "Three minutes!"

"Thanks," I said. I looked around as the ballad transitioned into a faster song. I didn't want to lose basking in the dreamy feeling of the moment, so I guided her off the dance floor and back to the high-top that held our drinks. I'd ordered her a birthday cupcake with a sparkling candle. Our server met us at the table and lit the candle while our new friends gathered around us.

"Happy birthday, Taylor!" We sang to her, and she blew out

the candle. I pulled the candle out of the frosting and held the cake-covered end to her lips. She sucked the frosting off, and I wanted to kiss off the remnants that didn't make it into her mouth.

Watching her, the urge to kiss her grew. I leaned forward, ignoring the snickering behind me, and kissed her thoroughly. I vaguely heard the conversation around us.

"C'mon, Damon. It's rude to stare."

"I was just thinking how I haven't kissed you like that in a couple hours."

"As you can see, I'm surviving without your kisses. Just barely, though."

Taylor giggled, and I upped the intensity of our kiss, trying to distract her from our friends' loving banter.

"We should fix that, honeybee," Damon said.

"We definitely should. Let's go make some babies."

"Yeah—wait. Babies? As in more than one?"

Damon's voice pitched, and I chuckled. I broke our kiss and grinned at Taylor, who released a melodic giggle. Her eyes were glassy, sparkling with warmth. She looked so . . . *happy.*

Shelby hooked her arm around Damon's and shrugged. "It could happen. My grandmother was a twin, you know."

I turned in time to see Damon's mouth gape open in surprise. We all laughed as she pulled him away. "Bye-ee!"

WHEN THE SUN'S RAYS WOKE ME HOURS LATER, I HEARD movement. I forced my eyes open and tried to memorize every detail of the scene in front of me.

A dappling of sunspots speckled the interior of our cabin. Dust motes danced in the light. From my high perch in the pullout bed, I could see Taylor's reflection in the mirror above the low dresser as she braided her hair. She hummed softly to whatever tune her earbuds delivered.

She caught me looking and waved but didn't turn around. I pointed to my ear, and she took out one of her earbuds.

"You're up early," I said, gathering my pillow under my chin. I waggled my eyebrows. "Got a hot date?"

"Oh yeah. With Matt. Floor mat, that is!" She giggled. "I want to get a workout in before we hit the beach."

"I'll join you." I sat up. "I could use your warm-up before I do *my* regular workout."

"You think you're funny. My workouts make football players cry."

"I'm not a football player. Hockey players are tougher." I crossed my arms, challenging her. I wanted to spend every possible minute with her. Time was moving too fast, and our vacation would be over in a blink. I couldn't waste a minute of this time we had alone together. I had a deep fear that getting back to reality would change things. And right now, everything seemed perfect.

"Oh, really? Let's find out then." She poked me in my chest. "Don't say I didn't warn you."

"Gimme all you got."

"I intend to."

Taylor's workout was no joke, and I found myself going easy on my lifting after her "warm-up." I watched her from the leg press as she lost herself in a yoga sequence.

I was ready to go when she finished, and an hour later, we disembarked at the tiny island owned by the cruise company.

We trekked over to the set of chairs and umbrellas we'd rented, and I ordered us drinks, watching from the corner of my eye as Taylor pulled her sundress over her head and tossed it over the back of her lounge chair.

"What, no skimpy bikini today?" I teased, taking in her tank and shorts set.

She snorted. "Sorry to disappoint you. I want to work out on the sand today. I need to get in some tumbling passes, which I can't do in the gym. Stay loose and fit for the competition, you know?"

"Too bad Nate's not here. He could throw you around."

A spark flicked in her eyes, and her eyebrows shot up. "Why don't you throw me around?" I opened my mouth to protest. "Nothing fancy," she assured me. "I could teach you the basics, and you could see what it's like. You can totally do it. You've got the strength, and I've got the balance. Perfect partnership."

An image of her on the sand, mangled and broken and bleeding, ran through my head.

"C'mon, Brewer. I know how to fall. Just don't drop me on purpose."

Never. "I would never drop you on purpose, Taylor." I hoped she heard the extra meaning in my tone. I meant it. Now that we were together, I couldn't imagine any instance that would break us up. Whatever hardships might come our way, we could work it out.

I was sure of it.

We sunscreened each other, and Taylor taught me the correct hand and arm placements for basic partner lifts. I picked it up pretty easily, and we drilled the same moves over and over.

"All right, I think you're ready to throw," she said. "We'll start easy. Hands on my waist." I stepped behind her, and she placed my hands where they needed to be and then covered them with her own. "Okay, now I'm going to bend and jump up. You guide me down, and on the up, I'm going to let go. That's when you'll get under me and catch my feet. Bring your feet in and hold mine tight at your chest."

"Got it." Sounded simple enough. She'd shown me a few videos that made it look easy, but I knew it wasn't.

"Five, six, seven, eight!" She bent, then bounced, and I grabbed her feet as she straightened in the air. "Awesome! That was perfect, Kingston!"

"Yeah?"

"Yeah! Okay, hold this position, and when I count again, bend your knees on seven and push straight up on eight."

"Got it."

"Five, six, seven, eight!" and she was straight up above my head. What a rush!

"How long am I holding you like this?" I shouted up to her.

"Ha! For the dismount, bend your knees, and when you push up, let go of my feet so you can catch me at the waist on my way down."

"That's it?"

"That's it! Bend on seven, toss on eight, then catch!"

"Can I call it?" I asked.

"Sure!"

"Five, six, seven, eight!" I caught her, and once I was sure she'd landed safely and fully intact, I spun her around for a bear hug. "That was amazing!" I laughed, giving her a squeeze and kissing the top of her head. "If I had to pick another sport —wow, that was fun!"

"I'm glad. Now back to work."

"Yes, coach!"

Up and down, up and down. I didn't know cheer stunting could be so fun. As I mastered each lift, she taught me a new one. We were heading back to our chairs when my phone buzzed. I glanced at it on the table between our chairs. My agent.

"Don't you need to get that?"

"Yeah." I picked it up, suddenly wishing I'd let it go to voice mail. I had a bad feeling it might not be what I wanted to hear. "Hey, Ron."

"Hey, kid. How's the Caribbean sun? I got your messages. Sorry I haven't called sooner. I was waiting until I had something to tell you."

"It's a nice change. Any news?"

He sighed. "Denver's left wings are solid, all four of them. They're not keen on you playing on the other side, and after the other night, there's buzz of you replacing Kriz as an alternate captain of the Voltage."

"Replacing Kriz? Where's he going?" Alexei hadn't mentioned being traded.

"Montana. His brother has been unofficially named captain of the new expansion team, and a deal was made for Alexei to sign to the minor team in Missoula, but he won't stay there. They'll bring him up after training camp to round off the defensive lines. He's a solid player and fits what they're looking for."

"I hadn't heard."

"He hasn't signed yet, and I'd guess he doesn't want to disturb you on your vacation. Listen, tell me what you want me to do. I can push for Denver, but it's likely you'll sit the bench or get sent back down, just like this past season. You won't get a good deal there, either. They need to shed salaries, not take on new ones, or they'll be over their cap. Just give me the word, and I can put feelers out, see who might be interested in a championship-winning left winger."

I turned to face the water to look for Taylor. She'd gone down to the tightly packed wet sand when I'd answered the phone. The beach was still pretty empty, so there was space for her to tumble on the harder-packed sand.

Taylor and me. We were *new*. I was assuming we were more than something, but what if it didn't last? What would happen to us if I left Colorado? "I guess push for Denver right now. My family's there . . . and my girlfriend." It was the first time I'd said it out loud, and I liked the way it sounded.

"Didn't know you were attached."

"It's new."

He cleared his throat. "Listen, kid, I'm going to be blunt. This is your career. Is staying with this girl worth risking everything you've worked your whole life for?"

I swallowed. My heart knew the answer to that question, but I had to be practical. I'd been waiting my whole life to get a contract to an NHL team. Hockey was the only thing I was good at, so my career—my life—was at their whim.

Would Taylor understand if I got picked up by another team? Traveling even half the time was tough enough on relationships, but being totally gone—relocating to another city—

for all that time, with only a few opportunities to meet up over nine months, would be hard. She knew the nature of the sport, but I wondered if she thought I was still vulnerable to the trades. Would she stay with me if I left?

And more importantly, how could I ask her to? I had no right to imply my career was more important than hers.

19

TAYLOR

*I*t was our last afternoon aboard the ship, and we'd hardly made use of the amenities, except for our couple's massage and a few trips to the gym. Kingston seemed distracted after the call with his agent, but I was confident if something was bothering him, he'd talk to me about it when he was ready. I thought an hour on the ice might help. I smiled as I remembered the first time I'd gone skating with friends on my birthday.

I spent some time thanking friends and family for the happy-birthday texts, then sent a group message to Shelby and Leda, remembering how they'd wanted to get Drake on ice skates. I'd been able to get us in for a reservation during the 2 p.m. skate.

I circled around with Leda and Shelby while Kingston and Damon supported Drake. I'd almost fallen a few times from laughing so hard. I'd never seen anyone so awkward on blades.

At some point, he seemed to get the hang of it enough to

stiffly stand on his own. Leda skated off to relieve the guys, and Kingston dropped back until he was next to me.

I patted him on the shoulder. "You're a good friend. It was sweet of you to help Drake."

"Poor guy. He needed all the help he could get."

He grabbed my hand and spun us around so that he was skating backward. I reached for his other hand and grabbed it, spinning us again until he was pulling me at high speed. I squealed in delight as the people blurred in my peripheral.

He was grinning at me stupidly, and I'm sure I wore a similar expression. I couldn't think of anything to say, so I just waggled my eyebrows at him. He spun us again and guided me into his arms, facing outward. His warm breath on my neck brought back the goosebumps and sent a shiver down my back.

"I've got a birthday gift for you," he whispered. "I was going to wait until dinner, but I don't want to." His hands dropped to my waist, and we glided to the gate.

"Then I don't want to wait." I pressed my lips to his. We found a bench and changed back into our shoes. With a quick wave to the others, we left the recreation area and headed back to our room.

"When did you have time to get me a gift?" I asked breathlessly as I tried to keep up with him. Where had he found this much energy after all the physical activity we'd exerted today?

"I'm sneaky like that." He flashed a grin and tugged me into the cabin, spinning me so that I was pressed against the door.

Kingston bent his head down, and I lifted to my toes to meet his lips. My calves began to protest, and I bobbled. He hoisted me up, and I wrapped my legs around his waist.

Slow and intentional, his lips worshiped mine. I closed my

eyes, savoring every light, feathery brush. And when I couldn't stand it any longer, I threaded my fingers into his hair and nudged him away. We stared at each other, and what I saw was emotion so raw, so real it was pure euphoria to bask in it.

When I came out of my love-drunk haze, I saw that the dresser was dotted in red rose petals. On a tray, a vase of red roses sat next to a champagne bottle chilled in an ice bin. A card leaned against the vase, and as I reached for it, Kingston scooped up the skinny, silver-wrapped rectangular box with a big red bow.

"Happy birthday, Taylor."

I took the box and sat on the bed, grinning stupidly. I was almost afraid to open it. I was sure it was jewelry, but I wasn't sure what that meant.

"Just open it. I hope you like it."

I untied the bow and slid the satiny ribbon off the box. Carefully, I worked at the paper until it released from the box. I wasn't normally a sentimental person, but a gut feeling told me I'd want to keep it as a memento. And the bow. And maybe a few dried roses, too.

I glanced up at him as I lifted the top of the box. He nodded, and I returned my attention to the gift. Inside, on a delicate chain, was a strip of silver tied into a bow.

"Oh, wow."

"You know, 'cause of your bow business and cheer and—"

I set the box down and launched myself at him. He lost his balance, and I caught him as we tumbled to the bed. He rolled me over and planted a chaste kiss on my lips before he jumped back up. "I love it," I assured him. "Thank you."

He kissed me again and reached for the card. "I got this for you before we left. I should have gotten you another card."

"You're the sweetest." I opened the envelope. Inside was a year's subscription for audiobooks. "This is perfect! Thank you!" Another kiss. I didn't think I could ever get enough kisses from this guy.

He pulled away and looked at me seriously. "I don't know how to do this, Taylor. I've never had a serious girlfriend. I . . . I want us to be serious. You want that, too, right?"

I nodded. "More than anything. I've never been in a 'grown-up' relationship either." I debated telling him why, then thought better of it. I'd never found anyone who lived up to the dreams of Kingston in my head. Maybe someday I'd tell him, but right now, I wanted him to know that I was happy—so happy—and that he was every bit as wonderful as I knew he would be. "We can learn it together."

He smiled. "You have no idea how happy I am to hear you say that."

"Oh, I have an idea." I kissed him again. "We should start getting ready, or we'll miss dinner."

I followed his gaze to the champagne and tapped him lightly. "How about we drink this while we get ready?"

I was glad our cabin had a split bath. He shaved while I showered, and I dried my hair when it was his turn. I was feeling shy, and though I'd seen him in next to nothing at the gym, and vice versa, I was experiencing a bout of insecurity.

When I'd zipped up my dress, I knocked on the bathroom door. "You can come out now."

I returned to the vanity-dresser and switched on my curling iron before rummaging through my jewelry pouch. I hadn't planned on wearing a necklace tonight, but Kingston's gift was perfect. I slipped on a faux diamond cuff bracelet and matching earrings, then held the delicate chain in my hand. It was beautiful, with what I imagined was a real diamond in the center of the knot.

"May I?" he asked. I glanced up and met Kingston's eyes in the mirror. "I've always wanted to do this," he said as I handed to him.

"You've never put a necklace on a girl before?"

"No, but my dad does this for my mom, and it, well, I've just always wanted to do it when I found someone I cared about the way he . . ." I lifted my hair while he fumbled with the hook. He brought the chain around my neck and clasped it. "You look amazing." His voice was barely a whisper.

I needed to lighten the tone before I suggested skipping dinner altogether. This was getting serious, fast. I was okay with that, but it was also a bit terrifying. "Wait till you see me with my hair curled and makeup done. I just might knock your socks off."

"You already did." I followed his gaze to his bare feet and chuckled. He kissed my neck. "I'll let you finish getting ready. I need to run a quick errand."

"To where?"

"I'll tell you later." I turned to receive his kiss. What was he up to?

20

KINGSTON

The lime hue of Taylor's formal dress illuminated her face in a way that made her glow from within. I couldn't stop looking at her, looking at me; her glittering eyes sparkled with the happiness I felt inside.

Man, did I have it bad. Kissing her the other night had released years of dormant desire I hadn't had the guts to acknowledge until now.

We met our tablemates at the elevator bank on the way to the dining room. I wanted to get a group picture that I could frame and give to Taylor. If everything worked out, this would be a birthday she'd always remember, and I didn't want either of us to forget one minute of it.

After pictures, I took Taylor's hand and followed our friends to our table. I'd arranged for a centerpiece of balloons, and each place setting had a cupcake with a lime fondant bow, the same shade as Taylor's dress, set in white frosting. The smile she awarded me made me feel less guilty about peeking into her garment bag yesterday.

She held up a cupcake in one hand and her phone in the

other. "Let's get a selfie for the fam." We took a few with different poses and expressions, and for the last one I turned her cheek my way for a kiss.

"Aw, look at you, Kingston!" Shelby praised. "Thanks for including us in the birthday celebration."

Hours later, as we slow-danced to even the fast songs, all I could think about was how the stars had aligned and everything felt right. I hoped to God I'd hear good news from my agent. Taylor seemed set on Denver, and it would be perfect if we were in the same city. Even if I had to spend another year on the Voltage, she wouldn't be far.

The party was still going strong, and I guided us closer to the wall as a group of couples about our age spread out to dance the Macarena.

"Whoa!" I stepped on something that felt like a wobbly stick. It knocked me off balance, and I heard squealing that sounded like my cat, Luc. Taylor's head flew from my chest, and she looked at me questioningly. "Sorry! Am I crazy, or did I just step on a cat's tail?"

"I didn't see a cat," Leda said, appearing next to me.

"No, no, no cat here," Drake said a little too quickly. I raised an eyebrow at him.

Out of the corner of my eye, I swear I saw a blur of gray fur run under the refreshment table.

"Drake, did you sneak a cat on board?" Shelby accused.

"Erm . . . no?"

"We should get going, babe," Leda said to Drake.

"Indeed." His eyes darted to where the not-cat had disappeared.

"If we don't see you at breakfast, have a wonderful trip back home. It was great meeting you and hanging out on our vacation," Leda said. She looped her arm through Drake's. "Ready to go?"

"We're going to head out, too," Damon said. "You kids have fun and don't do anything I wouldn't do." He winked, and Shelby rolled her eyes.

"We'll see you at breakfast," she said.

Taylor and I hugged them all anyway and made promises to keep in touch. After a few more songs, I suggested heading up to the deck for some fresh air.

"How about our balcony instead?" Taylor asked.

"Let's go."

She all but dragged me back to our cabin. Once inside, she took a play out of my book and backed me up against the closed door, pulling my head down to hers and kissing me like it was necessary for survival.

Our make-out session heated up, and she slid her hand up my chest. "Time for bed, roomie," she whispered.

I took her wrist and lifted her hand to my lips. "A perfect day."

"You're perfect. And I don't ever wanna be in that other place. That place without you."

I pulled her close. "We have our whole lives ahead of us. I don't want to rush one moment."

"Twelve years I've waited for you to kiss me, to want me. I want so much more with you . . . everything."

Her heated gaze made my insides weak. "I want everything with you, too, Lorikeet."

She sniffed, and her head fell into my chest. Her arms tightened around my waist. "Please don't call me that."

"Why not? It's what I call you."

"Because I hate it. Every time you say it, I just want to

scream. I hate my baby voice and calling me a bird's name is pouring salt into my wound."

"Wait. Hold up. You hate your voice? Why?" I was honestly stunned. All these years, I'd been calling her that. Sure, she'd complained about it, but it had always seemed good-natured. I thought she knew it was a positive thing. I really did love her voice. She must think I was the biggest jerk.

She crossed her arms and looked away with a shrug. "I sound like a little girl. Nobody takes me seriously. You calling me a lorikeet makes me sound like a chirping nightmare. I should have told you why I didn't like it, but I felt dumb."

I had to clear this up. "Babe, your voice is one of my favorite things about you."

She slowly turned her head back to me and squinted at me. "It—it is? What do you mean?" She looked both stricken and dumbfounded.

I reached out a tentative hand to cup her cheek. "Your voice is what makes you *you*. What makes people trust you and makes them feel like they're important and smart and loved. Why you're so good with little kids and when you coach me before games. It's an asset. I didn't know you felt that way about it. Honest. I've been calling you that for over ten years. It was a compliment. If I'd known it hurt you . . . I thought I was just teasing you. I promise, right now, I will never *ever* call you that again. I'm so sorry."

She closed her eyes and leaned into my hand. Water escaped from the corner of her eye and trailed down to my wrist.

Instead of answering, she wrapped her arms around my waist—tightly. "Thank you," she whispered. I didn't know exactly what she was thanking me for, but I sure as hell wasn't going to call her Lorikeet anymore.

LATER THAT NIGHT, I COULDN'T SLEEP, SO I CHECKED MY SOCIAL media. I didn't engage a lot, which meant I had a lot of notifications. I grinned when I saw several tags from Taylor's account. I clicked to see what she'd posted.

"Got me a boyfriend for my birthday. #socialmediaofficial!" followed by a heart emoji and all the selfies with me and her birthday cupcake.

I scrolled through the comments. Every single one was positive and supportive. A few mentioned how it took us long enough.

For once in my life, I didn't feel second best.

I was Taylor's one and only choice.

21

TAYLOR

I didn't want to get off the boat.

I woke up to my alarm at the crack of dawn. Luckily, we'd packed up most of our stuff and set it out for the porters, so I could swipe the snooze button.

It seemed awfully quiet. I'd gotten used to Kingston's light snoring coming from the berth. I squinted up toward his pull-down bed. The curtain was open, but he wasn't there. The cabin felt empty.

I remembered putting the moves on him the night before and then flipping out on him for calling me Lorikeet. It wasn't a big deal, not these days, anyway, but every time he called me that, I flashed back to my middle-school years. I wanted to be honest with him. I groaned and yanked the pillow over my head. "Stupid, stupid, stupid!" I yelled into the mattress.

I felt bad about throwing a fit about the nickname. I still couldn't believe he actually liked my voice. I knew he wouldn't lie to me, but it was just so hard for me to process after all the years of hating it.

The mechanical buzz at the door signaled its opening, and

Kingston's soft humming gave me hope that I hadn't botched our relationship before we'd even gotten it started.

The side of the bed depressed next to me, and he gently pried my hand from the pillow. "Taylor," he said softly. "Time to get up. You okay?"

I lifted the corner of the pillow and peeked out. "A little hungover and a little embarrassed." I sucked in my lips and squinted at him.

He grinned and kissed my nose. "Good thing I brought Tylenol, coffee, and kisses."

"Ugh." I turned my head back to the mattress. "You're too nice to me."

"I'm happy. Happiest I've ever been."

Ever?

I rolled over and patted the mattress beside me. "Happier than getting the scholarship to that fancy prep school?"

"Yup." He eased beside me and rearranged the pillows, careful not to transfer too much movement.

I snuggled up beside him and wrapped my arm around his middle. "Happier than getting drafted to New Orleans after playing in the juniors?

"Yup. Even if the Crescents bumped me down to the minors." He puckered his lips.

I stretched up to meet his lips, then rested my head on his shoulder. "Hmm. Happier than a Saturday night at home watching hockey with your cats?" I was sure I had him there.

He laughed, gently stroking my hair. "Are you there with us?"

"Yes."

"Then it's close. I'll have to think about it."

"Brat." I scooted a bit higher up the mattress, and our lips met again. Slow kisses were my favorite.

Remembering I hadn't brushed my teeth yet, I pulled away and slid off the bed. "We should get going if we want to say goodbye to our new friends."

He pulled me to him for another kiss. "I'll never get tired of kissing you."

"Me neither."

AFTER BREAKFAST, KINGSTON AND I SAID GOODBYE TO SHELBY and Damon.

"Be sure to keep in touch," Shelby made me promise. "If you're ever in Maine . . ."

"Same goes if you come visit Colorado." I hugged her tightly.

"Or we can do this every year," Damon suggested, wrapping his arms around both of us.

Shelby rolled her eyes. "He has *no* idea what he's in for if we have a baby next spring."

Kingston shook Damon's hand, and they did that bro-hug thing. "Let Drake and Leda know we're sorry we missed them."

With a bittersweet sigh, I slung my tote over my shoulder. Kingston took the handles of our carry-ons. "Ready, babe?"

"Ready."

"Bye, y'all!" Damon called after us, and I waved with my free hand. We took the elevator to the debarkation deck that led to the gangway and were hit with a blast of humidity. There was no breeze this morning, only a cool, light mist that surrounded the ship, sparkling like fairy dust in the bright sunlight. I tented my hand against the blinding sunlight and gave the ship a final look over my shoulder from the end of the gangplank.

"Keep moving! This way!" Helpful crew members waved lighted batons, directing us to the terminal entrance.

Disembarking was depressing.

Going through customs and retrieving our luggage didn't take long, and pretty soon we were seated on a shuttle to Orlando. It was still early, and check-in wasn't until four o'clock, so Chelsea and I had planned to spend the day at the Magic Kingdom, revisiting some of our favorite rides from when we were little girls.

"You still up for a day at the Happiest Place on Earth?" I asked Kingston as the bus turned out of the terminal.

"The happiest place is where you are," he said softly. "But if you want to go to Disney, I'm game."

"I do. Tomorrow I have to check in with the team, meet up with Kaycee, and move into her room. Speaking of the best roommate ever, she's bringing most of my supplies. Can you check with your coach if my packages have arrived?"

"Already did. He texted me last night when they were delivered. He's going to have one of his guys drop them at the resort."

"Awesome." I twisted to hug him. "Thank you," I whispered in his ear.

He kissed the side of my head. "Happy to help."

Best. Day. Ever.

We met princesses, rode rides, ate Dole Whip, and smooched for a photographer in front of Cinderella's Castle. As the last of the fireworks faded into the clear night sky, Kingston's arms tightened around me. I leaned back into him, and we just stood there, taking in the moment. I was hot, sweaty, and my hair took the term messy bun to a new level, but I didn't care.

I'd always been in love with the idea of Kingston. Now that I had him, it was no longer an idea.

It was the real thing. I was living out my happily-ever-after, and it was more magical than I could have ever imagined.

And I never wanted it to end.

KINGSTON

Fwwwhip. I locked the zip tie into place and passed the bow to Kaycee, who was in charge of hot-gluing a strip of gemstones to hide the strip of plastic connecting the covered elastic to the wide ribbon.

If anyone had told me last week I'd be at a resort making cheer bows with my best friend's little sister, her roommate, and my former coach's wife, I would've suggested they were one goal short of a hat trick. But with the extra help, she'd save enough time to go downtown tonight.

Taylor was already forming the next bow. We had a pretty effective assembly line going. Placing the ribbon on the cutting mat, inside facing up, she pulled the ends to the center to cross into an *X*. I slid a zip tie vertically underneath the middle of it. She pinched the ribbon together and added a covered elastic. I pulled the zip tie closed, and she fluffed the sides of the bow before I passed it off.

"This sure beats doing it myself with a needle and thread first. And I always make such a mess with the hot glue. You guys are the best. This is going much faster than usual!" Taylor flashed a grin at Kaycee and me.

"This is a fun break for me," Donna MacHolland interjected from the other side of the room, where she was steaming ribbon to vinyl strips of glitter with her heat press to prep them for Taylor. "We've had a lot going on, and I haven't had a chance to craft in a while."

"I really appreciate your help, Donna," Taylor said. "Such a blessing!"

"It's my pleasure. You've assembled a great team," she added, darting a glance my way. I shrugged.

"Happy to help as always, Tay," Kaycee said. "What I want to know is, why is *he* suddenly interested in making cheer bows? I'd have thought you'd have been on a plane home by now, Brewer."

Taylor blushed, her cheeks growing adorably pinker by the second. She was trying to be cool, but her blush and pressed lips gave her away.

"I knew it!" Kaycee squealed. "You two finally got together, didn't you?" Her green eyes darted from Taylor to me.

"Shh, Kaycee!" Taylor laughed. "Yes. Now calm down. I'll tell you all about it later. And check your social media for once!"

"You better not leave out any details." A look of understanding passed between them before she turned to me. "So what are your plans, Kingston?"

I shrugged. "I'm going to crash with an old teammate for a few days and catch up with some old friends." I glanced at the pile of bows. "We're going downtown tonight. If you ladies finish—"

"Yes, of course we want to come!" Kaycee spoke for them.

"We're going to be in a cheer bubble for two weeks, and I'd love to let loose a bit first."

I glanced at Taylor, and she nodded.

"Yeah, that sounds fun," Taylor said. "Can I invite Nate?"

"Sure." I shrugged. "Anyone you want."

"Great!" She jumped up. "I'll text him now. His plane lands in about an hour. What time will you head out?"

"We're meeting up at nine. Shaw O'Reilly is picking me up here about six, and we're going to grab dinner at a burger place on Church Street. If there'll be more than five of us, we'll need another driver."

"Nah, just us and Nate, if he wants to come," Kaycee said. "I know a few of the athletes from last year but no one I really connected with. That's why I requested to room with Tay."

"Great. I'll let Shaw know." My phone buzzed in my pocket. "That's probably him now. Can you ladies do without me for a few minutes?"

"Nope," Taylor said, then heaved a dramatic sigh. "But if we must . . ."

I winked and went into the hall. When I saw it was my agent, my heart skipped. *Please be the news I want to hear.*

"Brewer!" Ron sounded happy. That was a good sign.

"Hey, Ron. You sound like you have good news." The thumping in my chest mingled with the butterflies in my stomach. I almost felt sick with the anticipation.

"Oh yeah, kid. Not what you want to hear, but it's a no-brainer." I leaned against the wall, bracing for what he thought I'd accept instantly.

"That good, huh?" I tried to sound enthusiastic, but all that ran through my mind was that Taylor would be in Denver—and I wouldn't.

"Eight-hundred thousand average annual value. That's about Two point five million for three years. That's a half mill more overall than what we were asking from Denver."

I scrubbed the back of my neck. "Where?"

He laughed. "You'll never guess."

"Don't mess with me, Ron. If it's on the other side of the country, I—"

"Nope. Montana!"

"The Mavericks want me?" I wasn't surprised to hear they'd sought out Alexei, but two of us from the minors, from the same team, was definitely unusual.

"They do. It's not public yet, but Bennett MacHolland is about to sign on as an assistant coach."

"No kidding." I slid to the floor. Donna was just a few feet away on the other side of the door. Neither of them had even hinted to me about leaving Orlando.

So one of my best friends on the team *and* my old coach were going to Kalispell. They probably each put in a good word for me.

But Taylor was going to be in Denver.

It might as well have been on the other side of the country. We'd done a vacation to Flathead Lake when I was a kid, and it took us two days to drive there with all the stopping for snacks and bathroom breaks. I did some quick math and estimated it was probably about a fourteen- or fifteen-hour drive without stops from Palmer City. Probably a two-hour flight nonstop, not too bad. But . . .

Nine months of the year away for her. For three years.

Traveling for half the season would have been hard enough, but living all those miles apart? Could we survive it?

We could. I'd make sure we had the best summer of our

lives, and by September, it wouldn't matter where I'd be. If she loved me by then, and I hoped she would, it would be enough.

It would have to be enough.

"Kid, you there?"

"Yeah. Wow. That's . . . amazing. But how's that possible? Don't they just get one player from each team? The draft isn't for another month. I'm not on the Denver roster full-time, and if I was, first-year players are protected, right? How can they draft me?"

"Montana's general manager is already making deals. Denver is working on their protection list, and they know they'll have some of their star players exposed if they want to keep their current top lines. They can give the Mavericks options and bonuses. So you're the bonus here, plus a third-round entry draft pick. You played enough games to qualify for the draft *if* you keep your NHL contract, and you have more than two years of professional experience in the minors. That counts, so if you sign with the Voltage again, Montana can take you. They want you. Think you have great potential after your turnaround this year and your performance with the Edge."

It hit me that Taylor's coaching was the thing that would ultimately be taking me away from her.

"I think I'll take my chances waiting on Denver. Maybe Montana will draft a winger as their pick from the Edge."

"Not likely. They have their heart set on Černy."

"The backup goalie? How can they take both him and me?"

"You're not listening. Because they cut a deal. Pay attention. There are loopholes around every corner. Side deals and trades are a reality of this process, and deals will be made regardless, whether it be before or after the expansion draft.

The Mavericks are going to take two players from Denver, a current roster member and a prospect. Since they're already trading Alexei to their affiliate with the intention of bringing him up, that leaves opportunity for you."

"I see."

"Uh-huh. You sound like your cat died. I'm just saying, plan for it. You're available, and it might be your only option. And it's your *best* option. If you re-sign with the Voltage, Denver can bring you up—or let you go to Montana—or trade you somewhere else. You gonna bring your girl with you?"

I hadn't paid much attention to the expansion-draft rules because I honestly thought Denver would want me. Now it seemed like I only had one option if I wanted to keep playing. I glanced at Room 214's closed door and closed my eyes. "We're brand new, Ron. And she's got plans for grad school in Denver. So that's where I want to be."

"Ah. Makes sense now." He blew a breath into the phone. "Well, the Voltage are interested in keeping you around, even if there's a chance for Montana to swoop you up. Seventy thousand dollars for a two-way next season, with a chance to level up if something happens to one of their wingers. But, kid, honestly? This is a chance of a lifetime, and if the Mavericks come knocking, you should answer."

"I know." Adrenaline coursed through me as it sunk in that this was an official, full-time offer to play for a top-level team. I'd worked for this my entire life. The chance to play on a brand-new NHL team hadn't been my dream, but I couldn't brush aside what it meant. What about Taylor?

"Prepare yourself, kid. Re-sign with the Voltage when contracts are offered in July. And for God's sake, go talk to your girl."

"Yeah. Thanks, Ron."

I crossed my arms over my knees and dropped my head into them. This was both the best and worst thing that could happen to me right now.

Mon-freaking-tana.

23

TAYLOR

*L*ife was good.

No, life was *amazing.*

It felt amazing to be wanted by Kingston.

Amazing, amazing, amazing.

Kaycee hadn't minded Kingston crashing with us, and I woke up with his arm curled around my waist. After he left to take the call from his agent yesterday, he'd been quiet initially, but he was back to his happy Kingston-y self by the time Shaw picked us up, so I didn't want to pry. We'd have plenty of time to strategize for next season.

"Good morning," he whispered, and all my goosebumps stood at attention, waiting for orders. I shivered when his lips connected with my neck.

"Yes, it is." I grudgingly opened my eyes. Seven thirty. On the other bed, Kaycee was awake and smiling at her phone, her thumbs working furiously at the screen. "Who are you texting this early? It's still dark back home."

"Um . . ."

I remembered walking into the hotel and realizing she

wasn't with us. She'd hung back, and we'd sent Nate out to get her before we went upstairs.

"Is that Shaw?" I asked.

"His brother, Niall. Did y'all see him last night? He came late and left early."

"Yeah, he's the reason I'm on Shaw's couch tonight and not in the guest room." Kingston grumbled good-naturedly. "Good guy. You interested, Kaycee?"

She blushed. "He lives in Boston. I'm moving back to Biloxi at the end of the summer. But he *is* cute. And nice." She rolled onto her side to face us. "Kingston, did you know their little sister is here? She's on the US junior all-girl team."

"Nah. Small world."

"Totally. Anyway, Niall took vacation to fly in with Aisling and help her get settled. I told them we'd look out for her. They're coming to breakfast to introduce us to her and grab you, and then you three can head out."

"Sounds like a plan." Kingston's voice rumbled into my hair. It was a good thing he was leaving. His presence was doing funny things to me in the most distracting of ways.

WE SAID GOODBYE TO KINGSTON AND THE O'REILLY BROTHERS after breakfast. I hadn't anticipated how hard it would be to send him off. He'd still be in town a few days, but my practice schedule wouldn't allow me to see him. "I'll be home in two weeks," I said, but I knew it was going to be tough. "Video calls every night, okay?"

"Every night," he repeated. "And Taylor?"

"Yeah?"

"This was the best week of my life. Whatever happens, I want you to know that."

I brushed a curl off his forehead. "What do you mean?"

"About what?"

"You said 'whatever happens.' What do you think might happen?" I studied his face but couldn't read anything in his expression. My heartbeat picked up speed.

He smiled, but it didn't reach his eyes. His voice held a faint edge. "If I don't make it to Denver. If I get traded or signed with another team. This job . . . it doesn't make relationships easy." He looked away.

I pulled his face back to me. "I'm not looking for easy, Brewer. You're important to me, wherever you play. I'm invested. I don't care if you stay on the Voltage for another year. It's only an hour's drive home from Denver. I could even commute."

He pulled me close, and I tucked my head into his shoulder. "I'm just saying it's hard. I've seen it tear apart people who were perfect for each other."

"If it tore them apart, it wasn't perfect."

He smiled sadly. "Kick ass and take names at the competition, Taylor."

After another long kiss, I extracted myself from his arms. He squeezed my hand. "Call me tonight?"

"Count on it." He walked backward for a few steps until he reached Shaw. We returned their waves, and I stood there until they'd disappeared in the self-parking lot. I raked my teeth over my lower lip, trying to shake a feeling of foreboding.

"C'mon, Tay. You don't want to be late on the first day."

Kaycee looped her arm through mine, and her other through Aisling's. "You two are gonna have a blast!"

I was here, at the international championships. This was what I'd worked for the last ten years. I should be bouncing off the walls, not pining after a boy. That boy would be there when I got home, and we had nothing but time ahead of us.

So why did I feel like something wasn't quite right?

24

KINGSTON

"*D*ude, you are not okay."

I looked up from my phone's dark screen. Of course I wasn't okay. It was a few nights later, and I'd just hung up with Taylor. I'd be flying home in the morning.

But Shaw didn't know why I was upset. No one did, except Ron.

"It's nothing."

"Bull. You haven't been yourself the whole time you've been here. What gives? You've got a sweet girlfriend, and it's summer. So why the moping?"

I thought about it and decided to tell him about Montana. "But Taylor seems pretty set on going to grad school in Denver."

"Why? Because she thinks that's where you'll be?"

"I really thought I'd be pulled up permanently next season with Denver, especially with all the games I played for Denver when Moreau was injured. I went back down to the Voltage and led them in points. We turned around a crappy season and made it to the playoffs. I scored eight goals and got five assists over seven games. But it doesn't seem like it was enough."

"It's just timing, King." Shaw dropped onto the couch next to me. "One of those guys is bound to get drafted or traded or retire at some point. Moreau is almost forty, and he's slowing down. If I were you, I'd take the three years with the Montana NHL team. It's new, and it'll take a while for them to figure out who goes where. You're on a hot streak."

"Maybe. It's unlikely I'll see a lot of ice time with a team that doesn't know me, especially if they're already signing guys like Lukas Kriz." Three years might not seem like that long, but in a hockey player's life, it was an eternity. And without the guarantee of ice time, I'd be spinning my wheels behind the scenes.

Three years ago, I was playing in Orlando with Shaw. It didn't seem like that much time had passed. We picked up right where we left off. But Shaw's life had changed considerably. "What about you? You're getting up there in age. You've been here four years. You have a wife now and a baby. What are you doing next season?"

He didn't answer, but the corner of his mouth twitched.

"What? You can tell me."

"Well, we're definitely staying in Orlando. My wife loves it here. And it's a great place to raise kids."

"Kids? Is Katja pregnant again?"

"Yup."

"Congrats, man!" We grinned at each other.

"It was the end of the world when I got here. Can't really get much farther from Vancouver, eh? Katja and I were new then, and her brother had a fit when she decided to follow me here. Her citizenship issue was another obstacle that made it hard for us. We were separated for months, remember? Montana isn't as far away as Sweden, bro."

"No, I guess not." I frowned.

"If she's it for you, nothing will keep you apart forever. And who knows? Montana may surprise you, and you might never want to leave. I never thought I'd pick Florida after all the places I've lived. But my family loves to visit us, and I think my parents will move here after I tell them I'm thinking about retiring."

"Retiring?" I sat up. "Not moving up? I thought your dream was moving up to the NHL and one day playing for Boston?"

He shook his head. "Dreams can change. Like you said, I'm getting up there in age. I don't see a path to any of the Northeast teams. I don't want to go back there, anyway. I've had a great career, but I'm not at the elite level, and I've realized I don't like snow." He shrugged. "I might play one more year or maybe try coaching. My agent says a spot is opening up with the team."

I didn't comment on that. "That's cool, though. You'd make a great coach."

"I appreciate that."

He was quiet for a minute, so I changed the subject. "You know, you've totally lost your Boston accent. Your sister's is super thick. I couldn't understand half of what she was saying this morning."

He laughed. "Ay, now! Shut up, ya chucklehead!"

I put my hands up. "I take it back. The Boston accent is intact."

"An' you bettah remembah'rit."

"Whatevah, kid," I threw back at him. It felt good to laugh with my old teammate. But he'd given me a lot to think about.

"So the big question, then . . ."

I winced. I wasn't ready to decide yet.

"X-Box or PlayStation?"

25

TAYLOR

"*B*asket sequence again!" We were outside our hotel, on the grass, practicing in the building's shadow to escape the sun's harsh rays. The sun was finally beginning to sink into the horizon, giving us minimal relief from the humid Central Florida heat.

I shook out my arms and legs, which I could barely feel. It was going to be another ice-bath kinda day. I'd been struggling on my twist landing and was holding the whole team hostage from running the full routine. No one was leaving tonight until we hit it perfectly.

Nate patted my head as I took my place in the center of our stunt group. Exhausted didn't skim the surface of how depleted I felt. The last nine days had challenged me in ways I'd never dreamed.

I was glad I hadn't slacked on my workouts during the cruise, but I wasn't in peak shape, not like the athletes who'd just finished competing in the college championships. Luckily, there were a handful of post-graduates to commiserate with, including Nate. I wouldn't have gotten through this without him, I knew that for sure.

"You got this, Tay," he said, his big hands taking hold of my waist. "I'm behind you one hundred percent."

I snorted. "Literally." I placed my hands on the shoulders of my side bases and said a silent prayer for my landing.

"Set!"

I took a deep breath as Kane and Deshawn squatted into position. They were amazing athletes, and I'd learned to trust them when they'd flown in to Colorado Springs for our regional practices. Since January, team members had met regionally to practice stunts and choreography, so we were in good shape going into the event.

"Five, six, seven, eight!"

From the second my sneaker depressed onto the waiting hands of my bases, I was back in the zone. I felt no pain and relied on muscle memory through the pike-open-double. After the cradle catch, we immediately reset for a kick-double. The launch was smooth, and this time when my right leg shot out, I had plenty of time to twist, landing right-side-up in the cradle.

We landed it clean, and I couldn't contain my relief. Giddy and delirious, I launched myself at Nate. I couldn't tell if my cheeks were wet from sweat or tears, probably both.

The other groups were in a similar state of celebrating. "Did we all hit?" I asked our spotter.

He grinned. "Oh yeah."

"From the top!" Coach yelled. I fist-bumped Nate and ran to the edge of the mat to grab my poms and line up for the entry into our routine.

With two days to go before our first performance, the

team was killing it. Our elite skills, sequenced by our visionary of a coach, couldn't be touched if we hit zero deductions. The rest of the world hadn't quite caught up yet, but teams like Canada, with their partly inverted maple-leaf pyramid, and Chinese Taipei, who started their routines with a crowd-favorite basket sequence, would give us a run for our money.

By the time I got to my email that night, I could hardly move. I scrolled through, looking for messages that couldn't wait until tomorrow.

I forgot to breathe as I opened the email from the university in Denver. I must have groaned out loud, because Kaycee rushed over to ask if I was okay.

I couldn't look away from one particular sentence. *We are pleased to offer you a position as an athletic trainer with our athletic department...*

"Tay, that's great! It's not exactly what you wanted, but—"

"But it's what I'm qualified for." I sighed and pulled the screen on my laptop down to close it. I wanted to counsel. "Maybe if I'd paid the deposit sooner . . ." I also wondered what the other schools might have offered me if I'd accepted. But they were so far away.

"Well, that's your lesson to learn. You have friends—and parents—who are in a position to assist you. Don't keep shooting yourself in the foot. It's not a weakness to accept help. You give it all the time. Balance is key, you know?"

I bit my lip and sighed. I wanted to scream, but I didn't want to take my frustration out on Kaycee. "I get that. It's just that if I can't take care of myself, I'll feel like I've failed. I already have to work so hard to be taken seriously. Also, Chelsea got her grad program paid for, so I should be able to do the same. I don't want my parents to sacrifice and struggle anymore." My parents busted their butts to put Chelsea and me through college, and Chelsea had been able to get her master's program paid for thanks to her insanely high test scores and an assistantship.

She blinked at me. "You are anything but a failure, Taylor Ranford. I can't believe you just said that." She slid off the bed. "You know that's a choice your parents made. Cheer isn't cheap, either. They worked and paid for cheer and college because they wanted to. It's what parents do. Reach deep, and figure out why you feel like they should be done helping you. It's important."

I was too tired to argue, and when Kingston video-called me shortly after our conversation, he commented on it.

"You aren't beating my girlfriend's fierce body into the ground, are you?" he asked.

I melted a little hearing him call me his girlfriend and then forced a smile. "Let's just say lactic acid is a real issue right now."

"Ouch. Ice bath?"

"Yup."

"Tell me you can rest tomorrow?"

I laughed. "What's rest? We have a later start tomorrow, but I'll be finishing bows at six a.m."

"Making bows is not rest. Rest is when you do the opposite of beating your body to the ground. Recharge your batteries. Sleep. Cuddle with your boyfriend."

I smiled. "I'd love to be doing that right now."

"Me, too." His grin faded. "I thought I missed you during the season when you'd give me a pep talk over the phone before away games. This—this is a whole different level of missing you."

My hand started to shake, and my lip trembled. His confession overwhelmed me, and I hadn't been expecting to be overcome with emotion. He'd put to words what I'd been unable to. "I know what you mean," I whispered. "And I can't wait to see you in a few days."

"A few days," he repeated. "Already got my TV scheduled to record it, just in case." Kaycee and I had set our DVRs before we left as well, even though we knew everything would be online at some point.

"I should go. I'm spending the day with Adam tomorrow. I can't wait to show him the new comic."

I loved how Kingston's face brightened whenever he talked about his mentee. "Okay. I—" In my overtired delirium, I almost said *I love you* but caught myself. "I'll talk to you tomorrow."

"Night, babe."

"Night."

26

KINGSTON

*A*fter a great morning at the rink with Adam, I called Ron to check in. Still nothing new. He basically told me sit, wait, and stop complaining.

I was feeling sorry for myself and headed to Brewski's. The lunch rush was dying down when Brenna unloaded another round of drinks. She rested the tray against her hip. "King, you sure you're okay for another one? That makes four in two hours."

"Then I'm behind schedule." I glared at the bottle in front of me. I didn't hold my alcohol well, so Brewski's was the safest place for me. I knew I'd overdo it worse if I was at home with only Luc and Bourque for company, so I called Chelsea and Trask to meet me here, thinking at least one of them might be available for lunch on a Thursday afternoon.

Both were. Lucky me.

"This is your last one unless you eat something," Chelsea said. She and Brenna exchanged a glance. They'd been close friends since kindergarten and had made ganging up on me a sport.

Trask smirked. "I wish I had your problems right now."

"I know. This is what I've been working my whole life for. But Taylor . . . Man, she's been working hard for her dreams, too. I don't want to mess this up."

"Maybe not tell her until you're sure it's a possibility, then?" Chelsea suggested.

"I'm sure it's not as bad as you're imagining," Brenna said. "There are schools in Montana. Virtual classes. She could totally make it work."

"Yeah, I remember her researching a program in Missoula last year. But she's already put her deposit down for Denver," Chelsea said gently. "She'll lose it if she unenrolls, and grad-school application deadlines are now closed for the fall. She'd have to apply for the spring semester and hope to get in."

I ran my hand through my hair, tugging at the curls Taylor loved to play with. It made me miss her more, and I slumped lower into the padded booth, regretting my decision even more. Money issues I could help with, if she'd let me, but I couldn't change application deadline. And I couldn't ask her to wait another semester. "She didn't tell me that. I knew she had a few options, but I didn't know where those other schools were. It would be so much easier if we were both there. There's still a chance Montana won't want me."

"Also slim." Trask took a long pull from his beer. "MacHolland is likely the one pulling for you."

"He didn't mention anything when I saw him last week." I was going to push this denial to its limits. We all knew where I'd end up. That's why they were all here right now, wasn't it?

"You know he can't officially do that. Plus, you've played with both Kriz brothers. When you were pulled up for a few games your first season here, you played on that Magic Line with Lukas before he left to sign with Boise. If Moreau hadn't come back this year, after all those games you played, you'd have stayed, I'm sure of it."

I was sure of it, too. But that was the story of my life. Always second best.

Except with Taylor. She made me feel like I was someone. And now I was her someone. It hurt that I might have to leave her.

The bell on the door clanged with a violent force. Our gaze followed his to a tall, muscular man about our age carrying a toddler over his shoulder as he stormed into the restaurant, slinging a string of expletives toward the end of the bar where Kami was adding drinks to a serving tray.

Trask went rigid as he sat up. "Who the hell is that?"

The little girl he carried covered her ears, squirming in his grip as the verbal assault continued. He let her down gently as he neared the bar, and she ran to Kami, wrapping her arms around the surprised woman's legs.

"Damn," Brenna said, standing up. "He's not supposed to be here."

"Whoever he is, he can't talk to her like that." Trask set his beer down and started to stand.

"Down, boy. That's her ex-husband," Brenna warned. "She'll handle it."

"She shouldn't have to handle it. What a dirtbag. And saying all those things in front of the kid? What a jerk. She's so much better off without him."

"Which is why they're divorced. Just went through last week, but it's been a long time coming."

"I'm gonna—"

"Don't." Brenna's command was sharp. "I'll go see what I can do after he leaves."

Trask sat back down but didn't stop watching. Sure enough, a few minutes later, the man stalked back out, sans kid.

"He's just gonna leave her here?" he asked.

"Wouldn't be the first time." She sighed. "Auntie Brenna is going to see how she can help. If you guys don't need anything else?"

"We're good, Bren. If we can—"

"I'll let you know."

Trask glowered but didn't push.

"So . . ." Chelsea shifted. "Are you just going to sit around and sulk then?"

"What else is there to do?"

"Hello!" Chelsea gave me that look. "Go back to Orlando. Watch her perform and see if you can get MacHolland to talk."

Trask snorted. "She always boss you around like this?"

"Since the ninth grade." We laughed. "Yeah, I think I should. I don't know what to say, though, or how she's going to feel about it. Chels, I can't imagine the next three years without her. What if she only wants to be friends if I leave?"

She raised a brow. "You've managed to survive the last decade by being only friends. You're both still young. You have plenty of time."

"Says the girl who's my age and getting married."

She sat back. "You want to marry my sister?"

I shrugged. "Not now. I know this is new, but I feel like . . . I just know I don't ever want to be with anyone else. With her, it's like there's just no in-between, you know? How can there be?"

Chelsea pressed her lips together and reached over to pat my hand. "When your brother was at med school, I thought it'd be better if we were apart, but we were both miserable. I was so wrong, King. I wish we had tried to make it work. Remember?"

I did. Maybe Taylor and I could learn from our siblings' mistakes.

Maybe we wouldn't have to. I pulled out my phone to look for flights. "Which flight are you on?"

She pulled up her reservation, and I scrolled. "It's full. Looks like I can't get there until tomorrow night." I scanned the travel site, looking for anything that could get me there tonight. Nothing.

"That'll be fine. They'll make it to the finals. Just don't miss the second performance."

Not a chance.

I sent a text to Shaw. *Can you get me a ticket to Day 2 of the cheer finals?*

27

TAYLOR

*T*wo weeks had flown by. This was it. The last day of the event.

One final performance.

Representing the USA on a large co-ed team at this championship was surreal. We were ranked second going into the final round. Over ten days, our team had come together with a groundbreaking routine, featuring never-before-attempted elite-skill combinations. I'd been challenged beyond my scope of abilities. If we could hit zero on this last effort, we'd beat Canada.

Kaycee's all-girl team had won the gold in their division; Aisling's team had won the silver; and Nate and I placed fourth in partner stunts, so the entire USA delegation was on a high during team warm-ups. As we rotated stations backstage, my heart beat faster with the same adrenaline rush I relished when I was tumbling through the air.

"Let's bring it in!"

Nate lowered me to the ground, and the team gathered

around the coaching staff and spotters. We formed a tight circle and put our hands in.

"I know I speak for the entire staff when I say this," our head coach said. "It's been a privilege and an honor to coach this talented, dedicated team. Now let's get out there and show them who's the best in the world!"

"USA!"

I picked up my poms and slid my arm through Nate's. We were the second pair in line to run out, and I tried to peek past my teammates to see the crowd through the break in the curtain. A row of bare-chested guys halfway up the stands caught my eye. Each wore a painted letter on their chest, followed by a heart, that collectively said, "GO USA ♥."

"Look at those guys." I giggled to Nate.

He peeked out and then gave me a funny look.

"What?"

"*You* look at those guys."

"I can't really see them past Erik and Sharna."

"We'll move!" Erik shouted amiably.

As Canada's music ended and the athletes cleared the floor, I edged to the curtain and peeked out. G-O U-S-A—that was Shaw! How sweet, he'd come to see his sister and—OMG!

"You see him now?" Nate asked with a grin. "He's the one with the heart."

I smacked him lightly. "Lame." But I was smiling.

Kingston was here. And next to him, my sister. I'd have swooned if there had been time to fully process what that meant to me.

"Let's go!" Sharna scooted back in front of me as we were announced. I jogged out on Nate's arm with a renewed excitement. I didn't think I could get more pumped up.

The next four minutes passed in a blur. We warmed up the crowd with our patriotic chant of "red, white, blue" and then transitioned into our stunt groups. The music blared as the tumblers ran their sequences, and I lost myself to the routine. I flew through the air, successfully executing my three basket tosses, and as we built our pyramid, the energy emanating from the crowd amplified our own until it was all-consuming.

I chewed on my thumbnail while we waited for our scores. When we learned we hit zero, we lost it. Zero deductions on a routine was critical in every competition. The coach's strategy to have us practice in regional groups had paid off. By the time all of us got together, we'd nearly perfected our stunts, and no one could touch our difficulty level.

When Canada was announced as the runners-up, the crowd brought the house down. We'd done it! Nate lifted me onto his shoulders, and someone passed me a gold medal. I was laughing and crying and trying to position myself so I could see Kingston.

His arms were in the air, and his face was red from his screaming. I wished I was close enough to see his face, so I just blew him a kiss. When he blew one back, I pretended to catch it and tuck it in an imaginary pocket. Gosh, how I'd missed him.

HOURS LATER, AFTER THE AWARDS, CLOSING CEREMONIES, AND A whole lot of crying and hugging backstage, we boarded the bus that would take us back to our hotel.

I checked my phone for messages. Over a dozen new. I scrolled to read Kingston's first.

A heated flush crept up my neck as I read his sweet messages. The final one was a photo of a line drawing of a bow with a pom behind it.

Love the sketch! What's it for?

Just reminds me of you. Are you on your way back to the hotel?

Awww . . . Yup. Are you there?

Yeah. Hanging with Shaw's parents. Chelsea's here, too.

Can't wait to hug you!

Prepare for a long one. Two weeks' worth.

I'm ready!

As we pulled up to the lobby entrance, the bus had to slow to a crawl. A dim roar grew into a loud chant of *U-S-A!* and I couldn't believe what I saw out my window. I poked my partner, who was dozing next to me with his arms crossed. "Nate, look!"

He jerked awake, and I laughed. "What?"

"Outside!"

"Wow. That's for us?"

We joined in the chant as we filed off the bus and I searched the crowd for my people. It was well-lit, but in the sea of bodies, there was no way I'd be able to find them.

"This is nuts," Nate shouted. "Let them find us!"

I hooked my arm in his as the crowd parted to let the team through. I was too short to see past the people lining our path, though I craned my neck to try.

In the lobby, I saw him, standing on a couch that lined the wall, scanning the crowd. I was too short; he'd never see me.

"Nate!" I poked him, and he bent to hear me. "Lift me up so he can find us!"

My partner squatted down, grabbed me around the knees, and hefted me onto his right shoulder. I grabbed his left shoulder for balance and waved my right hand wildly. "Kingston!"

His head turned, and he jumped to the floor. Weaving through the people, his heated gaze remained on me, and I felt a thrill of joy knowing he'd truly missed me as much as I'd missed him.

I slid down from Nate's shoulder-sit and right into Kingston's arms. I wrapped my arms around his neck and pulled his head down for two weeks' worth of kisses.

KINGSTON

I pulled away from Taylor's kiss only because we were getting jostled in the middle of the busy lobby. "Wanna get out of here?" I whispered.

"Let me shower and change really quick."

"So this is how it is now, huh?" Chelsea said, but she was smiling. "See boyfriend, forget sister. See girlfriend, forget best friend."

Taylor hugged her sister. "I'm sorry! I just—"

Chelsea laughed. "I'm just teasing. My job is done. Congrats on your big win! And *this*."

"He's my big win," Taylor said, turning back to me. Those simple four words made up for a lifetime of finishing just short of a goal. After two weeks apart, she still wanted me.

I felt like the big winner tonight.

I'd hold off telling her about Montana until we got back home. I couldn't put a damper on our reunion by sharing possibly bad news when it might not even be a thing.

WE FLEW HOME THE NEXT DAY, AND THE DAY AFTER THAT I took Taylor on our first official date. It seemed backward, seeing how we'd been attached at the hip on the cruise, but I felt like I needed this memory for us. She loved zip-lining, but we'd never gone together.

I knew fancy wouldn't impress her, and I wanted it to be memorable. I'd booked the latest appointment available so that we'd be done just before sunset.

The thrill of jumping off the platform never got old for me, and seeing Taylor enjoy it reminded me of when we went snorkeling. She found so much joy in the simplest things, and I loved that about her.

As we followed the group up the trail to Brayden Pointe, which offered the prettiest views of Palmer City, I took Taylor's hand and slowed down so that we'd be at the end of the line. "C'mere." Her eyebrow lifted, but she didn't question me. We climbed up to the last platform, where we'd zip-line over Yanni Gorge. I twirled her until her back was pressed to me, and we had a perfect view of twilight over the depths below.

"Wow," she said breathily. "The sky is really on fire tonight. I've never seen so many colors in a sunset. It's breathtaking."

"It doesn't come close to you." I kissed her cheek and tightened my arms around her.

She turned and lifted on her toes to plant a kiss on my lips. Our helmets clacked, and we laughed and tried again. My skin blazed from the heat of her stare, and the ground shifted under my feet. I grabbed the rail to steady myself.

"You flatter me, Brewer." Her voice had a teasing edge to it, but she didn't smile, and when her fingertips danced up the skin of my neck, drawing goosebumps in their wake, I wanted to take her right back to my place and flatter her all night long.

TAYLOR AND I FELL INTO A ROUTINE OVER THE NEXT FEW weeks. We were both coaching during the day—me at the Plex giving private lessons to peewees, and Taylor at a regional cheer camp. We'd meet back at my place or hers—mostly mine, since she was a big fan of cat snuggles—and watch classic movies from the '80s and '90s.

Every couple of days, she asked if I'd heard from my agent. I think she knew I wasn't telling her everything, but when I re-signed with the Voltage, she stopped asking. The expansion draft was still a few weeks away, two days before the regular draft, and I was doing my best to keep both of the events out of my mind and out of conversations.

The night before the draft, we met Jackson and Chelsea at Brewski's, toasting Taylor's official acceptance to grad school. I was so proud of her.

Now if only the Edge would call me up. If I didn't hear anything, I still had a chance to make their roster during training camp in September. But, as it was only late July, all I could do was wait. And a lot could happen between now and then. I could be traded, loaned out to another team as far away as Europe, or my contract could be sold. The life of a minor league hockey player had never seemed so bleak to me.

The snug wasn't available, so Brenna sat us at a six-top table along the side wall, which had minimal views of the television screens. The expansion draft was the highlight on every sports station. All the sports channels were making predictions about what might happen tomorrow. Along with Lukas, three other superstar players, now free agents, had signed with the Mavericks ahead of the draft, and they counted for their former team's pick.

Luckily, the conversation was all about Taylor and her plans, so little attention was paid to the screens above our heads. The only thing that was said about Denver was that Černy going to Montana was almost a certainty. Taylor asked why he couldn't sign early, and I explained it was because of the terms of his contract.

About an hour into dinner, Jason and Lauren came in, and we invited them to join us. Jackson and I slid over to the chairs at the sides of the table so they could sit next to each other across from Taylor and Chelsea.

"You look like you need a stiff drink, Lauren," Chelsea remarked. Usually chatty, Lauren hadn't said a word yet. She looked tired. "You look too stressed for being on summer vacation."

"Yeah, the stiffer the better. My principal just switched me from teaching first grade to fourth grade. Our enrollment numbers were off a bit, and I was the last teacher hired. No one else wanted to move, so I'm it. I've got three weeks to learn how to teach fourth graders all the strategies they need for the state testing."

"Yikes," Taylor said. "I'd be freaking out."

Lauren shrugged. "Honestly, I almost expected it. I've taught first grade for five years, at three schools and in two states. I was lucky to find a same-grade position. It's rare these days for a teacher to stay in the same grade, at the same school, for their entire career."

"I'd think that would be a positive thing," Chelsea said. "To master a grade level. By doing the same one for years, you can get to know the age and recognize what works and what doesn't and who is really having problems."

"You can also get too comfortable," Lauren said. "The fourth-grade teachers I'm joining are decades older than me. They all started with the school when it opened, and I'm not sure what they're going to think of my modern teaching style or methods."

I thought about that while Brenna took their orders. "Can you get a job teaching first grade at another school?"

"I could, but I don't want to. It's going to be a big adjustment and a lot of extra work, trial and error. But there's so much I can learn from these women, and about kids." She rubbed Jason's shoulder. "I just won't be able to make it to as many games because I'll be in survival mode, taking it week by week."

"She's not one of those teachers who leaves when the last bell rings," Jason said proudly and leaned in to kiss her. She glowed at his praise and blushed after the kiss. "You know," he said, "I don't think Dr. Brewer would mind if you corrected papers in their suite."

I laughed. "She definitely wouldn't. Mom would probably tell you to invite your students along, though, and you wouldn't get much work done."

"That would make a great reading incentive! And I could get this guy"—she nudged him with her shoulder—"and some of his friends to make an appearance."

"Anytime," Jason said. "Especially if that's the only time I can see you on a game day."

Taylor made some suggestions on how to get and keep the attention of eight- and nine-year-olds, and I sat back, listening to the conversation but not completely participating in it. Lauren's perspective on adjusting was encouraging. I hoped with all my heart it was something I wouldn't have to worry about.

TAYLOR

I scooted out of cheer camp at lunchtime the day after we celebrated my grad-school plans. Kingston and Kaycee were helping me finish a bow order, and I wanted to get it done before we went over to Alexei and Ginny's, where some of the Voltage were gathering to watch the live stream of the expansion draft.

After my stomach rumbled, I suggested ordering pizza. As I scrolled through the online menu's options, an email notification flashed across my screen from the gym I'd made Nationals bows for.

"Kaycee! Oh my God!" I stared at the email. It had to be a mistake.

"What is it?" Kingston asked. He was wrapping toddler-size bows in tissue paper and packing them into the shipping box. Best boyfriend ever.

Kaycee peered over my shoulder at the screen. "Is that for real?"

"If it is, it's the end of my money problems. This will make a nice cushion for the fall semester. I could even afford to pay you to help."

She shook her head. "Trust fund, remember? I do what I want, when I want, forever and ever, amen. And since you won't let me pay for your school . . ."

I sighed. We'd been over this dozens of times. "Fine. I won't pay you. But at least pinch me."

"If you insist."

"Ow! Okay, okay." I laughed. "I guess it's real. Holy . . ."

"Yeah. They must have been really happy with the bows you made them for Nationals. New team bows for *twenty-three* teams. Yikes!"

"You want me to help with the design, babe?" Kingston asked.

I flushed, remembering the effects of his guiding hand on the cruise ship. "They're practice bows, so basically the same design, but I could *probably* use a consultation." I waggled my eyebrows at him.

Kaycee rolled her eyes. "Get a room."

"Hush! We're talking bow designs. They're just different centers for each of the age groups. Over five hundred bows! And they want them as soon as possible. Do you think we can get them done in time?"

"No doubt," Kaycee said. "Rush-order the supplies. At thirty bucks a pop, I'd totally spend extra to get your supplies here as soon as possible."

"Good point."

Kingston's phone rang. "I'll be right back," he said.

I wondered who it was. He didn't usually step out to answer a call. He'd seemed off the last few weeks. I wished he would trust me with whatever was bugging him. I'd have to know what was bothering him before the season started so we could strategize.

Kaycee and I were discussing the bow order when Kingston came back in. His smile didn't reach his eyes.

"What's wrong?" I asked. He glanced at Kaycee and shook his head.

"I have to go. Team thing just came up. I'll—I'll call you later?"

"Sure." I didn't push, because whatever it was, he'd been clear he didn't want to talk about it in front of Kaycee. "You want me to meet you at the Krizes' at seven thirty?"

"Yeah. Is that okay?"

"Of course." He kissed me goodbye, a long, slow kiss that made Kaycee repeat her suggestion of getting a room. I watched him go and sighed.

"You've got it bad, girl."

"Yeeeeeah."

She chuckled. "Order the food, and then let's finish these up. I'm starving."

We finished the bows, and after pizza and a shower, I texted Ginny to see if I could stop on the way to pick up any last-minute things. "Kaycee, have you seen my phone?"

"You left it charging in the kitchen, and it rang a couple times while you were in the shower," she called from her room.

"Thanks!"

I retrieved it and swiped. Four missed calls: three from Kingston and one from Chelsea. Text messages from each of them. There were more from Chelsea, so I opened hers first, figuring I'd call Kingston back after I read his texts.

Why aren't you answering your phone?

DO NOT be mad at Kingston or make him feel guilty about leaving.

Where are you? Did you already talk to him?

Kingston told me he hasn't spoken to you yet. So where are you?

Call me back!

What the heck was going on? Leaving? Leaving where? My apartment, to go to the team event, or somewhere else? I thought about his phone call and sudden departure. Who had called him about a team thing? What could come up suddenly?

He'd already signed his contract. The expansion draft, maybe? But that didn't have anything to do with him. Maybe Jason was moving up and they were gathering to congratulate him?

But he would have told me if Jason was moving up, wouldn't he? He'd be thrilled for his friend. That dread from a few weeks ago returned in full force. I was out of ideas. I swiped to open the missed texts from Kingston.

Hey, babe. Please call me. I'm so sorry if you saw the news first or heard about it before I could tell you myself. I didn't know for sure until I talked to our GM. I should have told you it was a real possibility that I could get drafted through a side deal so we could prepare for it. I just really hoped it wouldn't happen.

He got drafted? That didn't make sense. He was drafted years ago, right out of high school, and he'd just re-signed with the Voltage. What was he talking about? I scrolled to read the rest of the texts.

Please don't be mad.

We can figure this out, right?

Please call me when you read this. ♥

My hand was shaking as I exited out of messages. I pulled up a search engine and typed in "Kingston Brewer trade." Insiders had been leaking expansion draft picks all day, so maybe there was more information that could help me understand.

I gasped when I saw the first headline. *Bigger Sky Awaits: Voltage Top Scorer Kingston Brewer Traded to the Mavericks in a Surprising Side Deal.* The thumbnail of the video I didn't have the guts to play pictured Kingston high-fiving teammates gathered around him.

It was old footage from him re-signing with the Voltage, but it still stung.

"Tay, you all right?"

A lump in my throat the size of a puck prevented me from answering. I shook my head and covered my mouth with my free hand.

She leaned in. "Oh, damn. That's amazing! He finally made it to the NHL!"

"I know! I'm so happy for him." I swiped at my eyes. "But . . . Montana?"

Kaycee grimaced. "You didn't know?" I shook my head, and she put her arm around me. "You have to call him."

"I can't. I—why didn't he tell me this could happen?" My shock was turning to anger. He'd been drafted, but he hadn't seemed surprised in his texts, only sad. But he couldn't have known . . . could he?

What had his text said? *I didn't know for sure until . . .* Which meant he'd had to have known about it prior, and he hadn't mentioned it.

Yet he'd talked to my sister about it.

I think that's what stung the most. Why wouldn't he have told me this was a possibility? Asked me what I thought? I was his mindset coach! We were supposed to talk about these things. And I'd just sent all my money to Denver. I was locked in for a two-year program.

And he was going to Montana. *For three years.*

Where did that leave us?

Over a thousand miles apart.

How could there be an us?

I texted Chelsea to ask her to let Kingston and the Krizes know I wouldn't be going over for the draft. I couldn't think clearly, and I needed time to process all of this by myself. I was glad Kaycee and I didn't have the sports network that the draft was on so I wasn't tempted to watch the fanfare.

Kaycee rubbed my back while I stared at my phone. When it lit up, I jumped. Unknown number. I accidently swiped it the wrong way. Might as well answer it.

"Hello?"

"Taylor Ranford?" The voice was familiar, but I couldn't place it.

"Yes?"

"Adri Delicata here. You must be so proud of your friend Kingston! I was hoping to get a quote from his mindset coach for a feature write-up I'm doing on him. Hometown boy makes it big and all that."

My friend Kingston? How did this woman have my number but not know that we were a couple?

"How did you get my number?" I asked.

"I googled you. Love your cheer bows, by the way!"

"Thanks." I thought for a minute. "I'm incredibly proud of him. And I'm going to miss him so much."

"You sound like you really care for him. I noticed how you

looked at each other the night I met you. Did he ever get the guts to ask you out?"

"Sorta. He kissed me at a party, and that was that." I smiled. Why was I telling this woman about us?

"I've got to hear more about that kiss! Another time, though. Tell me, what advice will you be giving him when he moves up?"

The same thing I always told him. "That he's as good as he believes he is. That with a plan and clear goals, he can achieve anything. And to look out for the players who seem off and to encourage them, even if he doesn't feel it. They're probably hurting—physically or mentally—and need some grace."

"That's great advice. Can I hire you for my boys? Their mental state is a mess." She laughed. "I'm only half kidding."

"I'm not certified, but we can talk more if you want."

"Excellent. I'll be in touch. Thanks again."

"You're welcome." I hung up the phone and burst into tears.

30

KINGSTON

"*C*hels, did she say why she hasn't called me back?" I paced my apartment, phone to my ear, trying not to trip over Luc and Bourque as they chased me the length of the living and dining area.

"No, nothing. Here, I'll read you a couple of her texts that aren't too personal—I don't want to break the Sister Code—so you can get an idea where she's at. Let me put you on speaker."

I scooped up Luc and nestled him into my shoulder. He stretched and purred into my neck. From the floor, Bourque mewed his annoyance. "You're too heavy, and you don't stay still," I reminded him. He turned and flicked his tail, clearly annoyed with me.

"Okay. I sent her a bunch of texts asking her to call me and to not be mad at you. She has every right to be, though. You messed up big-time, King. You should have told her as soon as you knew there was a chance of you going to Mon-freaking-tana. When I said to wait, I didn't mean to wait until you got signed. I meant you shouldn't mention it until you knew it was a for-real possibility. You knew that weeks ago. You also knew Denver had to leave a couple of their stars exposed and that they were hoping to control who Montana took. Even I know they'd do just about anything to protect Caleb Carrier and Oscar Picard."

"I know, I know. So how do I fix it?"

"Sounds like time is your friend right now. She texted me, *I can't talk tonight. I need to think.* So I texted her, *You need to talk to him, Taylor.* She wrote back, *Why? He didn't bother to talk to me.*"

"Damn." My hold on Luc tightened, and he shifted. I bent to let him down, and he scampered off with an angry yowl.

"I texted her a few more times, and then I tried calling her. She wouldn't answer the phone, so I called Kaycee. She *still* wouldn't talk to me, even when Kaycee turned on the video and put the phone in front of her. She looked so sad, Kingston. I haven't seen her look that dejected since she found out her teammate died her freshman year."

This was worse than I thought. I'd hurt her, deep. How could I have messed up so royally?

"So what do I do? Just wait?"

"I think that's all you can do. Give her time. She cares about you. A lot. More than she wants you to know. But she just dropped every cent she has on grad school. This timing really sucks."

"But Chels—two point five million! I can send her to grad school anywhere she wants to go!"

"Not the point, and don't you dare tell her that. It's insulting. She's worked really hard to pay her own bills, and she's not looking for a sugar daddy who can solve all her money problems. Besides, Kaycee already offered, and she said no."

I pulled at my hair. "I'm going to go for a run. Please call me if you hear anything else."

"Time, King. She's just gotten a huge bow order to fill, and she's got one more week of working ten hours a day at that cheer camp. Let her get through that."

"Dammit! Should I call Nate? To check in?"

She sighed. "I don't see how it will help. Text her every day. Let her know you're thinking of her. Think of something to get her attention, prove that you're sorry. And time. If nothing else, time."

When I got back from my run, I sat on the couch staring at the blank television for a long time. The cats came and went. As the sun rose, light from the window behind me streamed into my apartment. I longed for the sunrises that woke us up on the ship. Taylor in my arms. Taylor beside me everywhere. Taylor standing in my hands on the beach.

I needed to see her. The emptiness I was feeling was agony. What if she never spoke to me again?

If you don't take the shot, you have zero chance of scoring.

What if going to Montana made me miss my shot with Taylor?

31

TAYLOR

*T*he grassy lot beside Brewski's was usually reserved for overflow parking for restaurant patrons, but today it was roped off for Kingston's going-away party. Ever humble, Kingston had insisted Alexei be included as well.

I parked my car on the edge of the paved lot and sat back in my seat to steady my nerves. I hadn't seen or spoken to him since the night of the draft announcement. Those couple of weeks felt like years. I had to talk to him today, but I didn't want to. Everything was happening so fast.

Kaycee took the keys from my hand. "I'll stick close, and you just tell me when you want to leave. Have a few drinks and relax. You got this, Tay. And I got you."

"Thanks, Kay." Kay and Tay. We were coming up on the fifth anniversary of our friendship, and I was going to miss her when she moved back to Mississippi. So many changes this summer.

I wasn't ready for any of them.

At least a hundred people of all ages were mingling and sitting around. Waitstaff from the restaurant hustled to and from the party, and Kingston's cousin Drew was mixing drinks for a long line at the outdoor bar. A backdrop with the Mavericks logo had been set up in the back corner, and a photographer was taking pictures of partygoers.

I craned my neck as we skirted around a line of kids at one of the bounce houses, but I couldn't find Kingston. "Drink line first?" I asked Kaycee.

"Absolutely!"

"Coach Taylor! You're here! Can you spot us? Auntie Ginny said no tumbling because she can't help because her back hurts—" I caught a whir of blond hair before two preschool-size heads slammed into each side of me, almost knocking me over.

I laughed as I caught my balance. "Of course, Klara!" I squatted down, and her brother, Kord, threw his arms around me, throwing off my balance for good. As my back hit the grass, the five-year-old twins climbed on top of me in a fit of giggles.

I looked up at Kaycee and grinned. "Wanna help?"

"Sure thing! But first I need to meet these sweet kiddos. Hi! I'm Kaycee, and I can do everything Taylor can do. Well, on the ground, anyway. I don't fly in the air like she does." She grinned and offered me her hand to pull me up.

"I'm Klara, and this is Kord. And that"—she pointed to a brown-haired girl with unruly curls standing a few feet away —"is our new friend, Ryleigh." She cupped her hands around her mouth and whispered loudly. "Can you help her, too? She's three and doesn't tumble *at all*." Klara emphasized the last two words, and it was hard not to laugh at her shocked sincerity. "I think she should start with a somersault."

"Of course we can," Kaycee said. "And a forward roll is a

good idea. I'll go introduce myself. I happen to be an expert at forward rolls."

I was grateful Kaycee offered to help their new friend. I wasn't in the right headspace to teach. Klara and Kord were more advanced, and drills were muscle memory to all of us at this point. We found a shady patch of grass behind the bar, and I knelt in the required position, holding my right arm straight out. Klara barely touched it as she executed her back handsprings, and I only had to push Kord's legs over a few times.

I was in the zone and lost in my thoughts, so I didn't hear Ginny approach until she cleared her throat. "Klara, Kord, it's time to let Coach Taylor get back to the party. They just set up a new bouncy house, and Uncle Alexei is looking for you to race. It's an obstacle course, and he thinks he can beat you. I wonder which of you is the fastest?"

"I am!" Klara said. "Come with us, Ryleigh." She took the little girl's hand, and the three of them ran off.

"Really, it was no trouble," I told Ginny. "They're great kids, and I'm not feeling very social today."

"You wanna just go, then?" Kaycee asked. "I meant it when I said we can leave anytime."

"I'm fine, for now. I need to wish him well." Kingston was at the backdrop now, acting goofy with his brother and cousins while Chelsea took pictures with her phone alongside the photographer.

"Alexei tells me he's miserable," Ginny said. "That re-signing with the Voltage was a gamble, but it was his best chance to stay here."

I lowered my eyes. I was still mad and hadn't let him

explain. "But he didn't tell me it was a possibility, even then. I don't know what to make of that."

"You'll just have to ask him," Kaycee said. "And let him speak, for goodness' sake."

"I can't even look at him without feeling like I'm going to cry. I don't want to make a scene here."

Ginny put a hand on my shoulder. "I'll see if Brenna can open the function room. Get some food, say hi to your parents, and I'll get Alexei to pull him away to meet you."

"Good plan," Kaycee said. "The Ranford and Brewer parental units have been looking over here quite a bit. Best go say hi before they realize something's up."

"They probably know. Chelsea isn't always the best secret-keeper," I said wryly.

"Even more reason to go check in," Ginny said. "I'll find you once I can set everything up."

Twenty minutes later, Ginny pulled me away from the quartet of camping chairs my parents and Kingston's occupied. Lucky for me, our moms were so distracted talking about Chelsea and Jackson's wedding plans that the effects of Kingston leaving didn't even come up.

Ginny left me at the door of the restaurant, and I went inside to wait for him. I didn't bother turning on the lights in the little room. The darker, the better, and the fading sunlight was sufficient. I sank into the padded booth along the back wall and folded my hands on the table. Now that I was alone, all I could think about was what I'd lost. I couldn't stop the tears and let my head fall into my arms.

A few minutes later, the seat beside me depressed and Kingston's strong arms pulled me to him. I buried my head in that stupid Montana jersey. I wanted to tear it off him and toss it in the smoker, but maybe if I soaked it with my tears, he'd think of me when he wore it.

"Hey, don't cry. We'll work through this."

"How?" I sobbed into his chest.

He didn't answer. I sat up and pulled his Voltage jersey from my tote bag and spread it number-side-up on the table. "I'm so proud of you, Kingston," I said, handing him a black marker.

His eyes shone as he took the marker from my hand and scribbled on the white number one. It was messy, but the words were clear. *To my #1 fan, Taylor. Thanks for always believing in me.*

"Thank you." I folded it up and put it back in my tote.

"Are we okay?" he asked.

"No. You didn't trust me enough to tell me about this. It must have been eating at you all summer. You re-signed with the Voltage, but even Ginny knew that was a gamble and a possible ticket to another team. Chelsea even knew about it." I rubbed at my eyes. "Why didn't you talk to me? I'm your coach. And your *girlfriend.* This is the kind of thing you discuss with your significant other. How come I didn't know you could get drafted from a minor league team to a brand-new NHL expansion team?"

"I'm sorry. I—I told you I didn't know how to do this serious-relationship thing. We said we'd figure it out together, remember?"

"Don't throw that at me," I said through my teeth. "Tell me how this happened."

He hung his head. "It's because I spent more than half the season on loan to Denver. The time I spent on professional minor league teams and the number of games I played for the

Edge qualified me for the draft. The Mavericks could have taken a star player, but they settled for the goalie and some side deals, which included me. Because of you, I got better, and a lot of important people noticed me when I played at that level. Then they hired my old coach from Orlando—"

"Coach MacHolland? Did you know about this when we were making cheer bows with his wife?" I stared at him, not wanting to believe he'd been keeping this from me *since the first week of our relationship.*

"Neither of them mentioned it, but yeah, I knew. My agent told me when I talked to him that day. I'm sorry I didn't tell you when I first heard it was a possibility. I wanted to pretend it wasn't. It was so unlikely. And then I tried to tell you so many times. I just couldn't. I was afraid you'd friend-zone me again."

"I wouldn't have," I whispered. "And I definitely wouldn't have sent all my money to Denver!" My tears spilled over again. I couldn't see a way to fix this. He said he wouldn't ever let me go, but that's exactly what he'd done.

"Please don't cry. We can make this work—"

"You keep saying that! But there's nothing to work if you don't want me to be with you for the next three years." I slid out of the booth, and he caught my hand.

"I can't ask you to not go to grad school and follow me to Montana! How selfish would that make me?" I shook my head. He didn't get it. "This was devastating to me, too. My own franchise rejected me. I didn't want to leave you. But it can be good. *We* can be good and make it work."

"I don't see how. We'll be living separate lives."

"This can't be the end of us. I'll do whatever it takes. We're just getting started. Please . . ."

Tears trickled out of the corners of his eyes, and I knew he'd meant every word of what he said. But I didn't see a path for us. I was going to Denver, and he was going to Kalispell. Neither of us knew anything about relationships or how to keep them together, never mind over distance and time.

I cut him off. I couldn't hear any more. I knew he was hurting, but he'd broken my trust. He hadn't come to me with the news that would impact our relationship more than anything else. "Three years is a long time. It's probably best we never really got started or super invested."

"But I *am* super invested."

"You clearly aren't. Not the way I'm invested in you. You said nothing about this to me. Not once did you give me the chance to explore other options, and you celebrated with me the night before you were chosen to go to Montana."

"I don't want you to compromise your dreams for me!"

He really didn't get it.

"Kingston." I squeezed his hand. "Sports psychology is a career. *You* were my dream."

"Taylor, I—I'm so sorry. There's always a possibility of me leaving or being traded. It's the nature of being a pro athlete. It's a job with a lot of travel. You know this. But you're right, it's a career. A job. And you're my life."

I couldn't believe he meant it. He was talking, but I couldn't hear his words. I felt like I was being suffocated in a fog of heartache, and I couldn't bear to be there another minute. I shook my head and stood up. "I can't. I have to go. You're going to be amazing in Montana. I'll watch every game, and you call me anytime you want encouragement or a pep talk." I took a deep breath to build up the courage for my next two words. "Bye, Kingston."

I speed-walked out of the room, through the restaurant, and out the side door so I could get to my car without having to go back to the party. Once outside, I swiped my phone to call Kaycee. "Please bring me home."

I shivered; the night chill had set in, and light rain added to my discomfort. Through the grace of God, I made it into the passenger seat before I crumpled, succumbing to the wave of grief that crushed me and pulled me under.

32

KINGSTON

I'd watched enough chick flicks to know I should have chased after Taylor when she ran out. I was so stunned all I could do was sit there. But I couldn't go after her. I didn't want to hold her back. She was going to be a doctor and help people, people like me. I wouldn't put myself before all the lives she could save.

"C'mon, King." Brenna poked her head in. "Get back out there. Everyone's looking for you."

"Not everyone." I sighed, pulling a napkin from the dispenser on the table. Shredding it seemed like a good idea. "Can't I just stay here? Or go hide in your barn?" Brewski's was on the edge of our family's original homestead. The empty barn behind the restaurant was set back by the tree line, and when the horses were relocated to my aunt and uncle's new property, Brenna asked if she could renovate it for when she started her wedding-planner business.

My cousin wasn't having it. She snatched the napkin bits from my fingers. "This is going to sound mean, but it's *your* party. Cry if you want to, but do it out there. Your parents are incredibly proud of you and somehow convinced mine to shut down the restaurant for half the day. We're all busting our asses to give you a celly for a job you've wanted your entire life. Hiding in here is a selfish snub to all the sacrifices they've made that led to this moment."

She was right. I slowly lifted my head. "You're right."

"Of course I am. And *no one* goes in my barn until I'm ready to overhaul it. Got it?"

"Noted." I slid out of the booth and followed her out.

One thing you learn early on as an athlete is how to compartmentalize. No matter what's going on in your personal life, you've got to check it before you step onto the ice, or it'll affect your game and bring the whole team down. I struggled with that after my move home, and Taylor helped me get that skill back.

Now I was using it to pretend everything was okay when it wasn't.

I almost laughed at the irony.

Putting on a show was something I could do. I avoided our parents and got through the rest of the party. The first thing I did when I got to my car was text Taylor.

Please, can I stop by? I'm leaving the party now.

Three dots lit up, then went away. They lit up again, teasing me with a response.

Are you there? I asked.

Sorry. Working on a bow order with Kaycee.

I could help?

A long pause, then *No, thanks.*

Just two words was all it took to deepen the crack in my heart. I started the engine and drove home, soaking in the familiar route from Brewski's to my apartment. The city lights shone bright behind me as I drove toward my complex against its mountain backdrop. I wondered if the moonlight glowed on the pines the same way in Kalispell as it did here.

Luc's yowling woke me from dreamless sleep a few mornings later. I opened my eyes to his morning headbutt greeting. Bourque jumped onto my back, turned in a circle, and plunked down, his twenty-four-pound attack knocking the air from my lungs.

Beyond the furry face licking my nose, the pink and orange glow of the sun rose behind the mountains. I longed for the Caribbean sunrise, the gentle waves lapping against the ship, the salty ocean air, and holding Taylor in my arms again.

This couldn't be it for us. I had to get her back.

"Sorry, buddy," I said, turning slowly to give Bourque a chance to readjust on the mattress. I failed to resist the urge to grab my phone and text Taylor.

Good morning. I miss you. I didn't expect her to be awake or to reply, so I put the phone back on the nightstand and got out of bed. Might as well start packing. I had errands to run, but nothing was open this early.

I was keeping my apartment. It was common for players to keep a main residence for the summer plus a temporary place in the city where they played. The job was unpredictable with trades and borrows, especially in the minors. My family was here. I'd be back in the off-season, and every chance I got, especially if Taylor was in Denver. I would fly home whenever

I could if she'd only give me a chance. I wasn't going to give up on us. I'd keep fighting.

Three days later, she still hadn't answered a call, returned a text message, or let me see her. I stalked her social media, but her only posts were from the cheer camp.

A week after that, the night before I had to move, Chelsea and Jackson brought over dinner from Brewski's. As they unpacked the takeout, I pointed to the stack of boxes against the dining-room wall.

"I'm not sure what I'll need or when, so I labeled them." I handed Jackson a printout cataloging the contents in the boxes. I wasn't bringing much with me initially, since I'd be staying with Alexei and his family until I decided if I wanted to buy or rent.

"You're such a dork." Chelsea took the list from Jackson. "What about your memorabilia? I mean, I can understand not taking your weights or books."

"I don't need it. It belongs here." Except for my Bobby Orr puck; that went where I went. Right now, it was one of my only connections to Taylor.

"*You* belong here," Chelsea said. "We're going to miss you." She pressed her lips together the way Taylor did, and my stomach clenched.

Jackson slung his arm around my shoulders. "We'll be up for the first home game." He glanced at the stack of boxes. "Just let us know which boxes to bring. You sure you don't want to bring more stuff with you just in case?"

"I can buy whatever I need," I remarked bitterly.

"I know three years sounds like a long time, bro. Chels has been a bug in Taylor's ear since the draft. You two saw what we went through when I went to med school. It was a mistake to break up. Some time together would have been better than no time. She'll come around."

"I just hope she's there tomorrow. I can't stand the thought of leaving without seeing her. I've given her space, but this . . . this is agonizing." I dropped onto the couch.

"Mrow."

Luc landed in my lap, and I stroked his soft fur. "And my cats are going to hate me." I smirked, thinking about the two carriers in my closet and the sixteen-hour drive.

"They still haven't forgiven you from the cross-country trek from New York, huh?" Chelsea sat down next to me and scratched Luc's chin.

"Doubtful."

They did their best to distract me, but I was glad when they left. I called Taylor and left a long voice mail. I wasn't sure if she was listening to my messages, so I also sent a text.

Leaving from Alexei's in the morning around nine. Can I stop by your place on my way?

I stared at the phone, willing her to reply.

I can't say goodbye to you.

I didn't want to say goodbye to her either. *So don't. We'll say see you soon.*

It's not a good idea.

I pulled at my hair. *Tell me what is a good idea, please. I want to fix this. Us.*

There is no us.

A howl rose from my gut, and I lost my cool, throwing my phone onto the couch. I grabbed at the bar separating the living room from the kitchen to steady myself and let the sobs free.

As the sun set over Billings the next night, I handed Lukas the keys to my SUV at a rest stop. He'd flown in to help with the driving so Alexei, Ginny, and I could get rest time. With four of us driving three vehicles—a box truck towing Ginny's car, plus Alexei's and my SUVs—we'd planned to drive straight through, but Klara and Kord had had to stop frequently for potty breaks.

Seven hours to go, and I was getting my first—and probably only—nap. After the cats stopped yowling, as they did every time the vehicle stopped and started, I drifted off. I dreamed about Taylor and our future together. I knew deep in my heart that she was my endgame and we'd sort this out somehow. I'd read Adri's interview with her dozens of times, and the pride and love she expressed for me made me think she knew I was her endgame, too.

Lukas tapped me a few hours later when we pulled into yet another rest stop. "I am going to drive the truck now so they can ride together," he said. His accent wasn't as thick as Alexei's, but when he was tired, it was more pronounced. "Ginny and the *děti* need sleep."

"I'm surprised they didn't want to stay overnight in Billings." Or take my mother's suggestion to leave at night so the kids could sleep through most of the drive, like we did on family road trips when Jackson and I were kids.

"Alexei is excited. Our parents and our sister, Petra, arrived last week from Prague. He is anxious to see them and pick a site for his house to build on the ranch."

The Kriz family had a longtime dream of owning a ranch in America, and Lukas had found a little one north of

Kalispell that would be a perfect spot for both his retiring parents and his younger brother's growing family. He'd made it clear to the league that he had every intention of retiring if he didn't play for the new team, and no one was surprised when the Mavericks scooped him up. He was still in his early thirties and had a few good years left. Boise was happy to let him go after his one-year contract was up and protect their other players from the draft, since he'd planned to leave anyway.

Two more stops later, and we rolled into downtown Kalispell as the sun was coming up. I followed the truck and Ginny's car through downtown, passing the new arena and construction zones for several new hotels and continuing north until the truck turned off Main Street.

Lukas's ranch wasn't far off the main road and currently had three homes on the property: a large farmhouse, a smaller foreman's home that he'd renovated for himself but was currently yielding to his brother and his family, and a hunting cabin at the back. The cabin would be the last to be renovated, and I thought about asking if I could rent it.

Mr. and Mrs. Kriz and Petra were waiting at the foreman's house. They pounced on Alexei's vehicle as soon as it pulled in, ignoring their son and daughter-in-law and going straight for the back doors. The sleepy kids perked up, and all of a sudden, everyone was speaking in Czech. Ginny's brother-in-law had spoken only Czech to his children, and Alexei had kept them fluent.

It didn't matter what language they were speaking, the love they had for each other was evident, and I watched with a pang of jealousy. Not wanting to marinate in my self-pity, I opened my own back door and checked on Luc and Bourque.

They glared at me through the cage doors of their carriers. I chuckled and lifted them out.

"Kitty box in guest room!" Alexei's mother shouted. "Upstairs, last room on left!"

I waved a thank you and went inside.

Mon-freaking-tana.

33

TAYLOR

*G*irls' Night Out at Brewski's was a bad idea.

Kaycee had lured me out under the false pretense of just the two of us drinking our woes away in the snug adjacent to the bar. Before Kami delivered our first round, Chelsea, Brenna, *and my mom* had shown up.

Out for dinner, Chelsea had said. *Fancy us being here. Can we join you?*

Uh-huh. Sure.

I sipped my rum runner in silence, stewing over how my life had gone from perfect to perfectly disastrous in only a week. Sulking was not my style, and I hated how my retreat appeared to be dramatic. Denver had been the most logical choice since I changed my major from exercise physiology to sports psychology my sophomore year. The program was exclusive and expensive and offered internships and place-ments close to home.

With Kingston playing so many games for the Denver Edge, everyone assumed they'd sign him on. The expansion draft had thrown an unexpected curve, and I would bet my life that he was struggling again with not being good enough, especially since I broke things off. I regretted leaving him the moment I walked out of Brewski's, but I still couldn't face him. And though I offered, I didn't know how I could work with him professionally. It just hurt too much, knowing we couldn't be together.

But it was for the best. And one day, maybe, the time would be right for us.

Kami poked her head through the snug's window. "Y'all want food?"

What I wanted wasn't on the menu, so I shook my head. Mom frowned. "You need to eat, sweetheart. Split the shepherd's pie bites with me?"

"Sure." Brenna's father had invented the recipe when he was in culinary school. Similar to a fried potato ball, but smaller, the bites were filled with corn, peas, diced carrots and onions, spices, and lean ground beef encased in mashed potatoes and then deep-fried. Served with a ramekin of gravy for dipping, they were perfect for picking at.

"If it makes you feel better, Kingston is miserable, too," Chelsea said, leaning into my ear. "He really regrets not telling you. Look, I feel partly to blame. I told him not to tell you until he was sure it was a possibility."

"But he didn't, even then." I sucked the last of my drink and pushed the glass to the middle of the table. "If I'd known sooner, I could have considered moving up there. He waited on purpose, Chels."

"He knows how important this is to you," Brenna remarked sharply. She'd always been like another big sister to me, having been one of Chelsea's besties in high school. "He wasn't here when you lost Nya, but he heard about it. He didn't want you to settle for anything less than the best program because you've worked so hard to make it happen."

"But so has he," I argued. "I'm not upset that he left. Well, I am, but not for the reasons you think. I'm upset because he didn't tell me it could happen or ask me to go with him. I'm upset because he discussed with my sister and his family and friends, but not with me. I'm upset because he just decided for both of us how this would go. And he assumed being apart for three years would be okay with me."

There, I'd finally said it aloud. That pain had been festering, simmering like a volcano ready to erupt, and now it spouted. I pressed my lips together, a desperate attempt to keep the lava from flowing.

"Was I okay for the years Jackson and I were apart?" Chelsea asked quietly.

We all knew the answer to that question. I dropped my face into my hands. I'd been so stupid.

"Oh, honey." Mom pulled me to her as my tears started to fall. I turned my head into her shoulder while I got myself under control.

"Have you listened to his voice messages?" Chelsea asked gently. Kaycee passed me a napkin as I sat up, shaking my head defeatedly.

"I can't. His voice . . . it just hurts too much."

"Listen now." Chelsea picked my phone up off the table. "We're right here, and you're already a crying mess. Rip the Band-Aid off and hear what he has to say."

"I think that's a good idea," Mom said, reaching up for the

plate Kami passed through the window. "Another round, please, Kami."

"Tell Drew to make a pitcher of that rum runner," Brenna instructed. "If Taylor doesn't finish it, I sure will."

"You got it." Kami passed in the last of the plates, extra napkins, and a pitcher of water. "I'm fixin' to leave at eight o'clock. My babysitter had an emergency, and she's bringing Ryleigh here, so Drew will take over when I go."

"Her dad can't get her?" Brenna asked, her expression hardening.

"Not tonight. He's got a late *meeting*." She and Brenna exchanged a meaningful glance.

"Ryleigh, the little girl from the party, right?" Kaycee asked.

Brenna nodded. "Kami, if you need to work, she can hang with us, and I'll trade my rum for water so I can take her home if she gets tired before you're done."

Kami's eyes darted around the booth. "If y'all are sure . . . thank you."

"Are you kidding me?" Brenna asked. "We all love that kid."

Kami flashed a smile and pulled a ring of keys from her pocket. "Her activity tote is in the car. Just in case."

"We got this." Brenna took the keys, and Kami hustled off.

"Listen to your messages, Taylor," Chelsea reminded me.

"I think I need another drink first. Liquid courage and all that."

Breanna poked her head through the window. "Drew! Stat on that pitcher!" He was at the window a moment later and passed it to Brenna with a salute. She grinned. "What? I'm his favorite sister."

"You're his only sister." Chelsea smirked.

"Details, details."

She poured the mixture and passed me a glass. I plunked a straw in and sucked it down in record time. The sweet, cool liquid was easy to consume, and a few minutes later, the desired level of fuzziness set in. I picked up my phone. Almost ready.

"Go on, honey. Want me to dial your voice mail for you?" Mom asked.

"No, I can do it." I rubbed my eyes one more time and swiped at my phone, typing in my password. *"You have eleven new unheard messages. To play your messages, press one . . ."*

Eleven messages? My gut clenched. I tapped the number one and held the phone to my ear.

"First unheard message." Kingston's tenor, wavering and clearly upset, entered my ear and seeped into my entire being. "Hey, it's me. Taylor, I don't know what to say. It happened so fast. I wanted to call you before the draft, but I couldn't even sneak away to the restroom. Please call me back. I want to come over and explain, in person."

"End of message. Delete, press seven. Save, press nine. More options, press zero." I quickly tapped the nine and waited for the next message. "Babe, please, call me back. It's been too long. I need to hear your voice, and see you. I have to leave soon. I want to spend every available second I have left in Palmer City with you. I can come over anytime."

Nine.

"Hey, Taylor, it's been three days. The only thing keeping me from going to you is Chelsea's death threat. I want to respect your space, but God, I miss you."

Nine. I missed him, too. So much it physically hurt.

"Hey, babe, it's me. I heard you're coming to the party. I—I can't wait to see you, hold you, kiss you, if you'll let me. It's been awful not seeing you every day, and I know you're hurting, too. I'm so sorry, and I want to fix this. Fix *us*. I'll see you there."

Nine.

"Chelsea said you aren't listening to my voice mails, so I don't know when or if you'll hear this. I hope it's after you've forgiven me. I hope you're listening and know how much you mean to me. It destroyed me when you left today. I've always felt second-best, Taylor. To my brother, to my teammates . . . until you. You made me realize my worth. You made me feel like I was special, on the ice and off it. That the trades were because of my strengths, not my weaknesses. You picked me —*me*, an undeserving jock who friend-zoned you because he thought his best friend's little sister was out of his league. What could a brilliant future sports psychologist see in a college dropout who skated for a living? But you saw *me*. And I saw you. And we felt complete. I know you're mad at me, but you can't dispute that we have something, and I want to fight for it."

Nine.

I covered my mouth, forcing down the guttural cries as I gasped to keep my breath even. Chelsea reached across the table to hold my free hand. The next few messages were more of the same. By the time the eleventh started, I was a blubbering mess.

"We made it to Kalispell. Got here early this morning. Drove straight through. Anyway, I thought about you the whole way. And there's a cheer gym not far from the turnoff to the Krizes' place. I think I remember your gym competing against them back in the day. Kali Elite All Stars? God, I miss you so much. I want to go back to the cruise, back to before I got that call from my agent, and do it all over, differently. I hate that we're apart. Just say the word, and I'll fly home first chance I get so we can work through this. I—I didn't want to say this over a message, but I need you to know. I love you, Taylor Ranford, and I will say that to anyone who will listen. I want to scream it from these mountaintops. Please don't give up on us."

Nine. The phone clattered to the table, and I turned into my mother's already damp shirt to cry the rest of my tears. Kaycee rubbed my back until I cried myself out. That last message was from yesterday. He hadn't called today, and that made me cry harder.

"You wanna go home, Tay?" Kaycee asked.

"I need to—I *have* to—I have to call him. I—"

"No need to explain." Mom pulled me close. "Kaycee, you stay here. I saw your eyes light up when you heard Ryleigh was coming. I'll just box up those shepherd's pie bites and take Taylor home. Chelsea, call me when you're ready to go, and I'll come back to pick you up."

"I can bring Chelsea home, Mrs. Ranford," Kaycee said.

"Perfect. We'll see you later then."

I hugged my sister and friends goodbye and followed Mom out. We didn't speak the entire ride home, and I was grateful she left me to my thoughts. She offered to come up, but I declined. It wasn't too late yet, and I wanted to call Kingston before he went to bed.

Not bothering with the lights, I went straight to the couch and tucked my feet up under me. Here goes . . . one ring . . . two . . . three . . . "This is Kingston. If I'm not answering, I'm sleeping or on the ice. Leave a message or send a text. P.S. Taylor, I love you."

I quickly swiped red to end the call before the beep. I'd been unprepared for that.

I needed to see his face, so I pulled up his social media. Pinned to the top was the photo of him and Alexei high-fiving teammates. Just below it was the selfie he took of us at Brayden Pointe. I was giggling at the camera, surprised when he'd turned his head to kiss my neck. The caption read simply, "My ♥ ."

I scrolled further. Picture after picture of us, posted today, with the same caption. He'd been serious about screaming it from the mountaintops.

Mountaintops. *Mon-freaking-tana.*

One thing about the cheer world, or any sport, really, at its highest level—it was a small world. I pulled up my email tab and sent a message to Kane, then powered up my laptop. He'd trained there and now worked for them as a tumbling and stunting coach.

The sports psychology program in Missoula had been a pipe dream until now. Kingston was worth it. Missoula was only two hours from Kalispell. The commute was doable. If I could find an apartment between the two cities, that would be even better. Classes started soon, so I'd have to call tomorrow to see if it was even possible to take classes without being accepted into a program for the fall semester. If it was, I'd swallow my pride and ask my parents for a loan.

If not, I was sure I could find enough work to keep me busy or take a couple of online classes if I couldn't go full-time. Heck, right now I'd learn to drive a plow if it meant being with Kingston.

He hadn't asked me to move there for him, but every sign pointed to that being what he wanted. I realized I had the power to make both our dreams come true, and I'd be damned if I threw away our future together.

There *was* an us. If he'd take me back.

KINGSTON

"*Nyet!* No, kitty!" The infuriated whisper-command of the little voice nudged me into the waking world. I opened one eye and peered at my alarm clock. *6:38 a.m.* A dusting of gray fur on the white sheet next to my pillow indicated the morning routine had begun.

Amused, I let my eyelid droop shut while the drama played out underneath my bed. Since I left the door open for Luc and Bourque, little miss Klara Havlova had taken that as an open invitation to "wake up" the cats. This morning was later than usual. Weren't kids supposed to sleep in during their summer vacation?

"Kord! Go around the other side. Push Bourque toward me. Luc is being naughty, so he can stay where he is. Bad *kočka!*"

I opened both eyes at this information, wondering what crime my smaller, less-docile feline had committed to get on Klara's naughty list. Kord's blond head came around, and his eyes widened in alarm at catching me awake. He was a quiet kid, content to let his sister run the show, but also a deep thinker, so when he did speak, people listened. I gave him a permissive wink, and he dropped to the ground.

"Okay, Kord, push! *Oomph!* I got him!" Kord popped up again and ran back to the other side. I turned over, wanting to see this play out. "Kord, pull my feet! I'm stuuuuuck!"

I met the boy's eyes again, and he shrugged. He tugged on his sister's feet, but she didn't budge.

"Let me help?" He nodded.

I pushed the comforter aside and knelt on the floor. Grabbing hold of Klara's sneakers, I pulled gently, guiding her onto her side as she resurfaced. Bourque squinted up at me from his prone position in her vise-like grip.

"Good kitty," I said, giving his belly a gentle rub.

Klara sat up. *"Kočka.* It means cat. I'll add it to your list." Klara had decided I should learn to speak Czech, and had taped a list of words she'd taught me to my door.

"Coach-ka," I repeated obediently.

"Almost!" She hefted Bourque over her shoulder. "Good try. Bye!"

I chuckled as they left the room, then peered under the bed. "You can come out now, Luc." He glared at me before tucking his face into his side. "Grumpy *kočka.*"

Not for the first time, I wondered what it'd be like to have a family of my own. Ginny's sister and her husband, a Czech hockey player, had been killed a few years ago in a car crash in Prague. Ginny'd moved the twins to Palmer City and took a coaching job at the Plex. A former Olympic skater, she and Alexei had met while his brother was playing in the Olympics. When Alexei was traded to Palmer City, they reconnected, and he stepped into the role of doting uncle from the start.

With their own baby expected in December, Alexei was on a mission to learn everything and make sure Ginny had help. He confided they'd tried to plan for a June baby, so that he could be home with her for the birth and the first couple months, but like many well-laid plans, it hadn't worked out that way.

I drove us to the rink that morning, and he was educating me about what to expect during the second trimester. I responded appropriately, but my thoughts were back in Palmer City. Even though I talked to or texted Chelsea every day, I still hadn't heard from Taylor.

"And this is why you are fighting for fourth line spot."

Alexei's comment jostled me to attention. I gripped the steering wheel tighter. "What?"

"Your head is not here. Your thoughts are miles away, and you will be riding the pine with me instead of playing next to Lukas like you should. I like your company, but you are better than what you are putting out there."

"There's no chance of me starting on the same line as your brother." I turned into the rink's lot and parked in the team's section. Amid the mix of sports cars and luxury SUVs, my midsize looked out of place.

"There is big chance. But you must believe it. Like last season."

"Last season I had Taylor. She believed in me."

He clapped me on the shoulder. "Listen. I almost lost Ginny because I didn't tell her how much I wanted her to be with me. I was also afraid that if I kept her from taking the job in New York, she might regret losing the opportunity."

"Exactly. How can I expect Taylor to leave when she's about to start her first-choice grad program?"

"You can't. You are not listening. Let *her* make choice. But you have to *give* her one. Invite her here. Two houses, we have room. And I will be leasing an apartment in Missoula for when I play with the Glaciers. She can stay there. Or get your own place. Show her you don't want to live without her."

I thought about his words for the rest of the day and decided to swallow my pride when I got home. Before I went in the house, I had one more message to leave for Taylor.

No voice mail this time. "Hey," she said. "I was just about to call you."

"You were?" My heart rate kicked up, hoping for good news. "God, I miss you so much. I have tomorrow off. Can I come and see you? I can fly in and—"

"No, that wouldn't be a good idea. I—"

"Why? Why wouldn't that be a good idea? Have you listened to my messages?" My free hand pulled at my hair, and I took a deep breath to suppress the growl that wanted to voice my frustration.

"Yes."

A flutter of hope interrupted the drumming in my chest. "Then why can't I fly home to see you?"

"Because I won't be there."

She wouldn't be there? "Are you already in Denver? I can go there."

"No, Kingston. I just landed in Kalispell. I was about to call a ride share to pick me up."

"You're here?" I shifted into reverse and peeled out of the driveway. "I'm coming to get you. *Please* . . . let me come get you?"

"O-okay." She sniffed. If she was crying, I'd make it my job to wipe her tears away and never cause them again. "I have so much to tell you."

TAYLOR

*K*ingston pulled up to the curb and jumped out without even bothering to close his door. Before the automatic tailgate opened all the way, I was in his arms and we were both a blubbering mess. He threaded his fingers through my hair and kissed every tear off my face. When I tried to swipe his away, he caught my hands and wrapped them around his neck.

The subtle scent of cedarwood tinged with floral notes and a trace of spice mingled with the salty scent of the perspiration beading at his temple. The aroma was heady, intoxicating, and overwhelmingly masculine. And I was lost in it.

I'd missed him so damn much.

"You're here. You're really here." He held me at arm's length, awe and sheer joy stretching his face wide.

I laughed. "In the flesh!"

"And the finest flesh it is!" He winked, and I snorted as he pulled me into another embrace. "Where did you find a Mavericks jersey?" He spun me around. "With my name on it?"

"At the airport. There's an entire shop dedicated to all things Montana."

"I didn't know. Are you going to let me sign it?" He raised a brow.

I pulled a marker from my jeans pocket. "I'd love for you to sign it." I turned around. I felt light pressure all over my back. "Are you coloring in the numbers?"

"In a way. Filling up the white space."

"Should I worry?"

"Nah. Okay. All done."

When I turned around, he was beaming, so I pulled my arms in and rotated the jersey so I could look down and see what he wrote.

Kingston ♥ *'s Taylor 4-eva* was written over a dozen times in all sizes over the one and six.

"Your teammates are going to razz you when they see this."

He shrugged. "Let them." He set his hands on my shoulders and leaned down for a kiss. I groaned in protest when it was over. "God, I've missed kissing you."

"I'm so glad you're here!" Kingston said, handing me an opened package of Gummi Bears. He'd de-sunshined them, and his face was all joy, just over what he thought was a visit. I couldn't wait to tell him the real reason I was here. I hoped he would be just as happy.

I turned in my seat. "How would you feel if I stayed here for a while?"

His fingers tightened on the wheel. "What about Denver?"

"Denver had one major flaw that I just couldn't get past."

"Yeah? What was that?"

"You aren't there. So . . ."

"You're killin' me, Taylor."

I grinned and told him about the program in Missoula, about two hours away. "And Kane—one of my Team USA bases—said I could always give private lessons at Kali Elite and maybe even help coach a team if it worked with my schedule."

"Wow, that's amazing."

"Yes, I'm pretty excited about it. Do you think the Krizes have room for one more until I can find a place?"

"Actually . . ." Kingston turned off South Main Street in the heart of downtown. We passed a football stadium before turning into a sleepy neighborhood. He stopped the car at the end of a gravel driveway that led to a charming brick and clapboard home framed by trees. A porch wrapped around the second level. I smiled, reminded of the stolen moments on the balcony outside our cabin on the *Dreamer*.

"For sale?" I asked, eyeing the sign in the yard.

Kingston let out a long breath. "Yeah. I found it by accident a few days ago. I'm thinking about buying it. I—I was going to stay with the Krizes, but if you wanted to, I mean, if you . . . Anyway, it's got amazing views of the Swan Mountains and Flathead Valley, and it's close to everything."

"It's nice."

"For us."

I slowly turned my head to look at him. "For us?"

He raised his arm and pointed to the right side of the home, which jutted toward the street next to the patio that filled out the left side. "That's a separate apartment, but it has connecting doors on each level. It could be a rental or office space."

I nodded slowly. "Looks like a good investment. You can

rent it to one of your teammates until you figure out what you want to do with it."

"Or you could work there."

I turned to him again. "I don't follow."

He cleared his throat. "Your bow business. It has its own kitchen, plus office space and a bedroom upstairs. And then maybe, in a few years . . . a sports-psychology practice? I mean, if we're—if I'm still playing for—um." He hung his head and smirked. "I'm really messing this up."

I held my breath and waited. I liked where this was going.

"I want you to live with me, Taylor. I know you like your space, and we're new, but we've known each other for a long time, and we were good roommates on the ship and—but if you stay, would you think about living here? With me? If I bought it? I could get you an apartment in Missoula, too, or Alexei said you could stay at his place for when you have to be on campus."

My lips spread into a slow grin, and then I lunged at him, throwing my arms around his neck and pressing my nose to his. "Yes! I don't care how long the drive is. I've got audio-books, remember? And there's *nowhere else* I'd rather be."

EPILOGUE: KINGSTON

Two months later

*H*ome opener. I sat in the locker room, half-dressed and waiting for Taylor to answer my video call. It was our tradition, a last-minute pep talk before I suited up.

"There you are." I grinned.

"Here I am! Kingston Brewer's number-one fan and mindset coach, at your service!" Her hair was up in its trade-mark ponytail with a giant glittery bow that matched the Montana colors. Behind her, I noticed Chelsea, Ginny, Klara, and Petra all wearing similar bows.

"You've started a bow trend," I said. "Nice."

"They're pretty cool, huh? And their favorite players' numbers are on them, too."

"I love it. You know"—I rubbed my chin—"if I play well tonight, they might want to talk to you. Would you be up for an interview?"

"If you score, I'll talk to whomever you want me to talk to."

"Hey, Taylor!" Alexei leaned over and poked his head into the frame. "I hope the *děti* are not giving you too much trouble?"

She grinned. "It was smart to get us a suite, I'll admit that much. Klara and Kord are everywhere at once. I made Ginny sit." She rotated her phone, and behind her, Ginny waved, a tight smile on her face as she held her belly and followed the kids with her eyes. Beyond the seats, my family and the Krizes were enjoying the buffet.

"You will get her plate, yes?" Alexei asked.

"Your mom is on it," Taylor replied. "I have a pep talk to give."

"That's your cue," I told Alexei.

He grinned. "Bye!"

I sat back and adjusted the phone's position. "Let's do this."

"Tell me why you need this pep talk."

I raised a brow, surprised at her question. "To set my mind and focus on the game. And because if I break our tradition and we lose, it'll be your fault, and I wouldn't want you to have to shoulder that kind of responsibility."

She snorted. "You people and your silly superstitions." She shook her head. "You don't need me, Kingston. Admit it."

"But I want you," I rasped.

She sighed dramatically. "Yeah, yeah, I know." A chuckle escaped, and she couldn't hold a straight face. "All right. Goals for tonight?"

"To score." I waggled an eyebrow.

"Be serious!" she scolded with a laugh.

"I am. My goal is one goal, and an assist if I get the opportunity. But I want the goal."

"And how are you going to get it?"

"I've practiced with my line and studied my opponents. I'm prepared, which allows me to think and act quickly."

"And?"

"And I'm good enough." I heard the determination in my voice. She made me end with those words every time, and tonight, I believed them.

NEAR THE END OF THE SECOND PERIOD, WE WERE STILL TIED AT zero. Seattle's defense was making it difficult to get decent shots off, and the goaltender stopped everything we slung at him. I was playing on the third line with Jacques Harfleur, acquired from New York, whom I had played with in the minors before he moved up, and Anders Nilsson, a center who'd been drafted from Seattle. I knew how important it was for Anders that we score against his former team.

When I'd told the PR department about my plan, they were all over it, but in order to make it seem realistic, I had to get a goal in the next four minutes and thirteen seconds. Otherwise, my interview at the close of the period wouldn't make sense and would potentially take the spotlight from a player who was more deserving.

With just under two minutes to go, we got our opportunity. Černy made an incredible stop in goal and passed the puck to Alexei to clear it. He sent it toward center ice, where Nilsson was waiting, and we crossed over the red line together. I set myself up to receive his pass, and when the puck collided with my stick, I fought to keep it.

Seattle's goalie fidgeted just inside the crease, and I didn't hesitate to pass it to Harfleur, like we'd done in practice. He shot it backward to Huff, who sent it back to me, and it was in the net before the goalie realized I even had it.

I glided across the ice, hands in the air, looking upward toward the family's suite. They were on their feet. A rush of joy filled me, and I hardly registered the high fives as I tapped gloves with my teammates on my way back to the bench.

When the horn signaled the end of the period, I hung back, letting my teammates file out to the locker room before I made my way to the end of the bench for my interview. Swapping my helmet for a Mavericks ball cap, I put it on backward and pulled on the headset.

"Everything in place?" I asked, reaching under the bench. My hand closed over the small box taped to the underside, and my heart kicked up a notch.

Sarina, head of the team's public relations, nodded. "She's making her way down right now."

"Brewer!" I looked over at the familiar voice. Adri Delicata strode toward me, mic in hand. "What, you think I was going to miss this?" She winked at Sarina. "Thanks for calling me."

I grinned, a bit dazed at the surprise. "You two know each other?"

"Our boys play together." She waved her hand. "Let's get this started. We've got the countdown. And there she is now! Fifteen seconds."

If you don't take the shot, you have zero chance of scoring.

I took a deep breath and sent a smile in Taylor's direction as she was guided to sit next to me on the bench. Her eyebrow quirked with interest, but there wasn't time to explain. Sarina had told her the press was interested in her strategies for helping my mindset, and that was true. She didn't like being the center of attention, so her agreement to do this was crucial to my plan. I was elated when she consented to be on camera.

"Three, two, one." Adri grinned and launched right into her questions. "So glad you're with us, Kingston. Can you talk to us about your strategy for tonight? How did it feel to score the first goal in franchise history for this new team?"

"It felt amazing." I smiled, reached for Taylor's hand, and laced my fingers through hers. "Our strategy tonight was simple. Take shots, and if you don't have one, pass it to a teammate until someone does." I turned my head to Taylor and looked her straight in her beautiful blue eyes. "My dad is always reminding me you miss every shot you don't take."

Adri went on when I didn't say more or turn back to her. "And that's exactly what you did. Tell me about your mindset going into this home opener and what you did to prepare mentally for the game."

Taylor smiled in encouragement. *Here we go.* "I have someone who's always reminding me that I'm good enough. That I have the skills and have done the inner work to achieve any goal I set."

Adri cut me off. "Taylor, pleasure to see you again. You've known Kingston since you were kids. What is it that makes him an ideal candidate for your coaching?"

Taylor pressed her lips together, and I knew she was choosing her words carefully. "Kingston is one of those people that pours his whole heart and soul into things that he cares about. Working with him is a joy for me because he takes my advice and applies it. You were in Palmer City last year—you saw him go from struggling on the minor league team to sliding right into the spot on the Edge and coming back home to kill it for the Voltage. He's got the heart of a champion. He just needs to be reminded of it regularly." She looked at me, and the admiration and love were enough to melt the whole rink.

"Excellent, excellent," Adri said. "And Kingston, would you agree with her assessment?"

"Oh yeah." I grinned. "I'd agree with anything she said. Taylor is the smartest, most beautiful person I've ever known, inside and out. She talks about my heart and soul, but one thing I learned is that neither are complete without her. *I'm* not complete without her. She makes me want to be better, so that's what I aim for." My free hand closed around the box under the bench.

Taylor swiped at her eyes and smiled. "That's how I feel about you."

"I'm so glad to hear that." My voice broke, and I forced back the lump that suddenly made it hard to swallow. "I love you, babe."

"I love you, too." We locked eyes, and I slid off the bench onto one knee. There was no turning back. We were on the Jumbotron, live television, and sports radio.

The gasps around us became white noise as I tuned out everything except the surprised face grinning back at me. "Taylor. You're the heart beating in my chest and the soul that fills me with everything that's good. You're my sunshine on a rainy day and my pizza and beer when we lose a game. Your spirit, your love for others, and your dedication to making people feel worthy of love and success impacts everyone who meets you. *And* you love me. Me." I shook my head, still incredulous.

"Well, you are pretty cute," she said, eliciting laughter from the arena.

"That's true," I said, chuckling. I grew serious again. "I'll never feel worthy of you, but I'd like to try. Will you marry me?"

The white noise grew to a din as the crowd waited for an answer. Taylor nodded, but her words weren't what I was expecting.

"On one condition," she whispered. Another collective gasp from the audience.

My heart pounded. "Name it."

She stroked my cheek. "You *are* worthy. And I want to hear you say it. Tell the world. I'm not better than you. Don't hold me on a pedestal. Let's conquer the mountain of life together, equally. Imperfectly, but perfect together."

"I'm worthy," I whispered.

"And I will marry you and love you with all of me, forever."

I slipped the ring on her finger, and we laughed, tears ribboning down our cheeks. I stood up and pulled her in for a kiss before realizing how bad I smelled, but she didn't say a word, just rested her head on my chest. I looked back to Adri. I wasn't sure what I was supposed to do next.

Even Adri was crying. "That was beautiful. Thanks for letting us"—her hand swept the arena—"be a part of your special moment."

I gave Taylor one last squeeze as we posed for a picture. "I have to get to the locker room."

She smacked me playfully on my backside. "You've won my heart, number sixteen. Now go win this game."

"Count on it."

Thanks so much for reading *Cruising on Ice!*

You're invited to the Ranford-Brewer double wedding!
Sign up for my newsletter at KerryEvelyn.com to get the
password to my Freebies page, where you'll find this bonus
epilogue and so much more!

Want to read the love stories of the couples featured in the
book?
Love on the Ice: Alexei & Ginny
Love on the Beach: Damon & Shelby
The Beachcomber's Buccaneer Bounty: Drake & Leda

Christmas on Ice

Look for **Christmas on Ice**, Book 2 in the Palmer City Voltage series, and add it to your Goodreads "Want to Read" list!

Kami Spencer has no plans for romance ...

After my divorce, I made two rules:

1. Never date guys with first names for last names.
2. Never date guys whose jobs require travel.

And definitely don't marry them.

I'd like to think I learned from my past experiences. But Trask Emerson feels like a mistake I might have to make ...

Also by Kerry Evelyn

Crane's Cove

Love on the Edge

Love on the Rocks

Love on the Beach

Love on the Fly

A Night at the Inn: A Lizzie Borden Short Story

The Cotton Candy Caper: A Fall Carnival Story

A Night in the Passage: A Crane's Cove Short Story

The Fisherman Nutcracker: A Whimsical Christmas Story

A Night in the Cabin: A Crane's Cove Short Story

A Second Shot at Love: A Second Chance Romance Novelette

A Home for Christmas: A Sweet Southern Christmas Story

Cat's Paw Cove

Moon Mist Manor Book 1: Christmas at Moon Mist Manor

Moon Mist Manor Book 2: Love Overrules the Lawyer

Moon Mist Manor Book 3 The Beachcomber's Buccaneer Bounty

Palmer City Voltage

Love on the Ice: A Hockey Romance Novelette

Cruising on Ice: A Sweet Friends-to Lovers Hockey Romance

Christmas on Ice: A Sweet Holiday Hockey Romance

Sparks on the Ice (Subscriber Bonus)

Melting the Ice: A Sweet Late to Love Romance (Late to Love Anthology)

Celebration on Ice: A Sweet Second-Chance Romance

Crushing on Ice: A Sweet Wedding Romance

Once Upon Academy

Birds of a Feather (Prequel)

Bird's Eye View (Once Upon Academy Volume 1)

Phoenix Rising (A Once Upon Academy Duet)

Nonfiction

City Nights (How I Met My Other Anthology)

Fenway: A Beacon of Hope (How I Met My Other 2 Anthology)

The Believer's Journal for Everyday Faith

The Advent Experience Keepsake Planner

How to Binge-Write Your Novel

ACKNOWLEDGMENTS

Thanks to all the families and coaches at Fire & Ice Cheer Allstars, Uprising Cheer Elite, and UKnight Training Center. It was a privilege and honor to be part of your programs and for my children to have opportunities to experience what true sportsmanship is under the guidance of coaches who had the right mindset and cared more about their athletes first and foremost. It was a bonus for my kids to learn from nurturing coaches and college and world champions at a young age to set the best kind of foundation. The examples you modeled inspired Taylor's journey to work hard on the floor and to become a sports psychologist to support others and make an impact.

To my hockey experts Kat, Las, Andrew, and Mike—I thought I knew a lot until I started writing this one! Thanks for being just a text away and helping me get the details just right!

So much gratitude to the early readers—Tonya, Laurie, Pam, Becki, and my mom, Judy—who muddled through the POV twists and expansion-deal turns at various stages of messy draft—I appreciate you so much!

To my writer friends, crit partners, and editors who also read the mess, supported me trying something new, and put up with me fussing over every little detail, thank you! Chelsea, Stephanie, Megan, Angelique, TJ, Jill, Brenna, Lila, Frieda,

Corrine, Candace, Lauren, Chris, and Nicole, you bless me infinitely!

To Anthony, Kailyn, and Nicholas, thank you for your grace with the hours this takes from you, the YOYO dinners, and all the stuff you do so that I can work my dream. I love y'all to infinity and beyond!

ABOUT THE AUTHOR

Kerry Evelyn is the author of the Crane's Cove series, #sweetresortromance set in Coastal Maine, the Palmer City Voltage #sweethockeyromance series, and several short stories that span multiple genres. She's also a Guest Author for the Cat's Paw Cove romance series, a writing instructor, and a contest judge. A native of the Massachusetts SouthCoast, Kerry changed her latitude in 2002 and now calls the Orlando area home. Fueled on faith, Dunkin' iced coffee, and a love for people, including her amazing family, Kerry loves (in ever-changing order) books, boy bands, cats, hockey, sweet drinks, taking selfies, traveling, and the madness of getting the stories in her head onto the page.

Website:
KerryEvelyn.com/links
Reader Group:
Facebook.com/groups/CranesCoveCrew
Facebook.com/KerryEvelynAuthor
Twitter.com/theKerryEvelyn
Instagram.com/KerryEvelynAuthor
Bookbub.com/authors/kerry-evelyn
Amazon.com/Kerry-Evelyn/e/B077LWTYXJ
Goodreads.com/author/show/17348375.Kerry_Evelyn

Love on the Beach

*T*he eyes glowed from the middle of the road, two silver disks reflecting the moonlight.

Shelby's breath caught, and fear trickled down her spine. She slammed the brakes of her father's Jetta. The tires screamed as the car came to a violent halt. The eyes continued to stare, mocking her.

Only a deer. It scampered into the trees. Her heart thundered as it hit her how close she'd been to a serious accident, but only God knew the number of her days.

Shelby shuddered and steered the car onto the shoulder. Her fists gripped the wheel. She breathed in, then out, long and slow as she'd been taught years ago. After a few minutes, her heartbeat slowed and became regular.

Red-and-blue lights flashed in her rearview mirror. *Are you kidding me?* It was late, and she'd just delivered a trio of twenty-somethings to their homes after they'd imbibed too much at the pub. Her fingers closed around her mother's diamond-embedded silver cross hanging around her throat. "Not this week, God," she murmured under her breath.

She wiped her tears and debated reverting to her "pastor's daughter" mask of pleasant face and voice. The handful of cops stationed in the cliffside town of Crane's Cove, Maine, knew her, and she knew them, and they knew why she was out late at night. She'd become a designated-driver volunteer for Paddy's Pub & Grill as soon as she turned eighteen. Her father didn't like it, but he understood her need to do it.

The fear transformed into agitation as the police SUV pulled up behind her. She tapped her fingers on the wheel, mouth set, jaw tight, and glanced at the clock. She had to be at the diner in five hours. *Just perfect.* "Keep it together, Shelby. You know these guys."

Or did she? She rolled down her window and squinted into the side mirror. The bulky shape of the approaching officer was similar to Will Donovan's, but he had left weeks ago for FBI training. As the figure approached, his easy swagger registered and sent off alarms in her head. None of the other officers in town were in that good of shape. In fact, that particular shape almost reminded her of—

NO. WAY.

"You *moved* here?" Shelby spat before the officer could ask for her license and registration. "Why?"

Damon Saunders, dubbed Atlanta's Hottest Bachelor by the *Peach Gazette*, stood before her in all his muscle-hugging uniformed glory. His eyes met hers and his stone-faced cop expression transformed into the most swoon-worthy, genuine grin she'd ever seen. He recognized her.

Don't stare, don't stare. She fought the magnetic pull and struggled to look away from his flawless light-brown skin and dark eyes illuminated by his flashlight. Resolute, she crossed her arms, tilted up her chin, and stared straight out her front windshield.

"Yes, ma'am." His deep baritone drawl prompted a shiver. "Seemed like a nice place. You also came back after being gone, right? Why?"

"Turned out city life wasn't for me. And please, don't call me 'ma'am.'" After six years of back and forth between Boston and Crane's Cove, including a year of interning at what was supposed to be a humanitarian-focused publication, she'd toughened up and learned what she didn't want to do with her life. She'd come home with a master of fine arts to her small town on the Acadian Coast. Now she was working part-time at the diner to supplement her freelance work while she figured out her next move.

"Seems we have something in common, then."

"I'm sure we have nothing in common." She didn't want to have anything in common with him. She was back home for the summer only, to regroup and refocus, and so far, everything was going according to plan.

She didn't have time for dating, no matter how interesting or hot the man was.

"I'll bet we do. Music, for example. As I recall, you crashed my cousin's wedding with the lead singer of the Harbor Lights. How'd you manage that?"

"We went to high school together. She used to sing with me at my dad's church." Shelby shrugged.

"See? Another thing in common. I used to sing at church, too."

Wonderful. She sighed, rolling her eyes.

Shelby met Damon through friends when he'd been a guest at the town's Cliff Walk Resort for his cousin Matt's wedding a month ago. He didn't hide that he was charmed by the small town—or that he was interested in getting to know her better. The guys crashed the bachelorette party, and, in a moment of weakness, Shelby had let her guard down and allowed him to pull her onto the dance floor. He was sweet, smooth, and smokin' hot.

The heat between them sizzled, and he surprised her by twisting her into a deep dip as the song faded out. As the final note played, they'd locked eyes. He'd lowered his lips for a gentle kiss before twisting her back up. Freaked out by how it had affected her, she'd bolted to the parking lot before he could ask for her number. As she sat in her car waiting for her friends, she went over all the reasons she couldn't get to know him better and vowed unsuccessfully to never think about him again.

So much so, she'd insisted on working the night of the wedding to avoid him. In any other time, in any other place, she might be interested—not because he was Mr. September on the Atlanta PD's charity calendar Yeah, she'd googled him. But there was more in those eyes than just pretty specks of light. She couldn't fight the draw, and she was glad when he went home to Atlanta. Out of sight, out of mind.

But now he was here—and she didn't know where she was going. The idyllic New England coastal town was fine for vacationers and townies who wanted to remove themselves from the ugliness of the world. Not for her. She wanted to make a difference, and she couldn't do it here. Here, in this small town, she couldn't make her mark on the world. Here, there were memories of her mother everywhere she went. Here, it was too painful.

"Well, get it over with," she said through her teeth. Her jaw remained clenched, and she held her posture so rigidly that her friend Kat's great-aunt would have been proud.

Damon rested his elbows on the open window ledge. She leaned away from him. "Get it over with? You got someplace you're supposed to be?" Any closer and he'd be invading her personal space.

"Home. In bed." Her cheeks heated after she spoke those last two words. She cringed. Oh, the things his easy southern drawl conjured in her mind. She swallowed. "I have to be at work early."

Damon shifted his weight to his left arm and peered at her. "Mmhmm. Well, you were speeding pretty fast when that deer came up on you. And your center backlight is out. I suppose I should write you a ticket or give you a warning, but I already feel like I'm on your bad side." He pressed his lips together. "I'm new in town and I want to be your friend. What do you say?"

Shelby whipped her head toward him, incredulous. "Are you bribing me? Aren't I the one who's supposed to try to get out of this?"

He grinned. "Did it work?"

Is he for real? Shelby let out a long breath. "Fine. Thank you. I will try to be pleasant when I see you around town."

Damon's grin stretched wider if that was even possible. *Look away, Shelby. He's everything you don't want.*

"Sweet! That's all I ask." He stood up and tapped his hand on the window ledge. "You have a good night, Shelby Porter. See ya around."

Shelby nodded and waved half-heartedly. Her tongue turned to jelly. She couldn't have spoken if she tried. Thank God he didn't notice her puffy eyes or flushed checks, or if he did, that he had the decency not to mention it.

Damon pulled into the diner as the sun's first light painted the horizon.

She wasn't kidding. She did have to work early. Shelby's car was parked along the side of the refurbished train car that was now the Cliffside Diner.

He wasn't stalking her, not really. He was just hungry after his first overnight shift at his new job, and the diner was the only place open. And yeah, he was hoping to see her again.

He'd looked for her at Matt and Lanie's wedding and was disappointed when he'd learned she was working. But then she'd strode in with Macy Wells, lead singer of the Harbor Lights, whom she'd convinced to sing the bride and groom's song. Once Macy started singing, Shelby was gone again.

And so was he.

Damon couldn't pinpoint what drew him to her. He was easygoing and friendly. Shelby was wound tight, cynical, and didn't waste any words. But he knew that was just for show. He'd seen her interact with her nephew, Noah, and it was contrary to the act she presented to everyone else. He closed his eyes and imagined her regarding him with the degree of warmth she bestowed on the little boy. He wanted to know why she barricaded herself behind a series of protective walls, and how he could break through them.

His eyes roamed over the old chrome-and-maroon railroad car that had been converted into a diner and reflected on the difference in working overnight in Crane's Cove versus the graveyard shift in Atlanta. Here, he'd sat by the side of the road for most of the night. Every hour or so, he cruised around town, checking the neighborhoods and familiarizing himself with the streets and layout. In Atlanta, he often went an entire shift without a break. He'd stocked his car with protein bars and a cooler of bottled water, and then he'd gone straight home and collapsed at the end of his shift if he wasn't required to put in overtime.

Damon shuddered thinking about his last job. He was so proud when he made detective. Despite five years on the force and seeing the worst of humanity, he couldn't have imagined the degree of cruelty he would come across while digging into the crimes he was assigned to.

That last bust was his breaking point. His boss granted him time to process the trauma, and he'd cashed in his vacation time to fly up to Crane's Cove to visit his grandmother. Meemaw was enjoying her summer away from the heat of Savannah, as well as helping to plan Matt and Lanie's wedding. He got to know some of the locals and began to think he could fit in here. Dread had consumed him each time he thought about going home to Atlanta and his job.

That was a month ago. Meemaw had sensed he wasn't in any rush to return, and when she learned that the police force in the little town was down a man, she'd suggested he apply. On a whim, he did, and he was surprised when he received the call requesting an interview. He'd flown back up last week and was already at work. Now he just needed to find an apartment. The extended-stay hotel in Winter Harbor was nice, but he couldn't live there forever.

He jogged up the steps to the diner and opened the door. "Hey, Ms. Sadie," he called out to the matronly woman filling sugar containers behind the counter.

"Look at you!" she clucked. Sadie set the sugar down and lifted the countertop at the end so she could approach him. She reached out and straightened the flap on his collar. "Yes, sir, you will fill my Will's shoes just perfectly. I'm so glad you took the job. Here, have a seat anywhere you like." She gestured to the empty restaurant. "How was your first night?"

"Mostly uneventful." He took a seat on a stool at the bar,

trying not to be obvious as his eyes scanned for Shelby. Sadie went back around to her side of the counter. In less than a minute, he was staring into a hot cup of coffee with a menu beside it. "Night and day from Atlanta."

"I'd imagine so. I'm happy to end up here after life's adventures," Sadie said. "Did your Meemaw tell you that I was with the FBI?"

Damon's eyes widened. "No. Makes sense though. You must be crazy proud of Will."

She beamed. "I am. He's working hard, but it's no picnic. I'm glad he was able to take his girlfriend on vacation between jobs. He won't get another one for a while." Sadie leaned in and raised her voice for the benefit of those in the kitchen who might overhear. "I'm retired, but I assisted when your cousin's wife was abducted." She shifted her gaze toward the windows in the swinging doors that led to the kitchen. "If you're waiting for the muffins, they should be out any minute." She lowered her voice. "I worked some cases that rattled me to the core. The worst ones were the children." She shook her head. "You can't imagine how creative some people can get when it comes to making babies suffer."

"I can. I have nightmares about it." He raised his eyes to hers. An understanding passed between them. "I don't mind the night shift. It's easier for me to sleep during the day."

The door to the kitchen opened. Shelby stopped dead in her tracks as she caught his gaze. The tray of muffins shifted in her hands as she steadied herself.

"Mornin', Shelby!" Damon sipped his coffee and winked.

Shelby avoided his eyes and set the tray on the counter. "Good morning, tough guy." She opened the clear glass cabinet and loaded the muffins into it.

Sadie glanced between the two of them. "Seems you two already know each other. Wonderful! Shelby, be a dear and grab his order for me? I'll finish up the baking."

Damon fixed his eyes on her as she slowly arranged the muffins on paper doilies in the cabinet. He moved his head around to catch her eyes, but she kept them down.

When she finished, she took a spiral pad out of her apron pocket and finally looked up. His heart thundered in his chest as Shelby flipped her long bangs to one side. Her almost-black hair was highlighted in lighter tones and pulled back from her face in a long slick ponytail that trailed over her shoulder, accentuating her high cheekbones and tanned skin.

Her words came out in one breath. "Today's special is a French crepe with pears, walnuts, spinach, and brie, with or without eggs. Comes with the diner's famous fried potatoes and your choice of toast, cheese roll, or English muffin. Add a side of bacon, sausage, or ham for two dollars more." She blinked at him three times and then held his gaze.

Damon hadn't heard a word she'd said. "Sure, I'll try that." He handed her his menu.

She blinked again. "Toast, cheese roll, or English muffin?"

He pointed to the muffins in the case. "One of those, please."

"And did you want to add a side?"

"Of what?" He knew he was staring. He couldn't help it.

She sighed. "Bacon, sausage, or ham?"

"Bacon, please."

"Egg or no egg?"

"Egg whites, please."

Shelby raised a brow, made a notation on her notepad, and disappeared into the kitchen. She returned with a small plate that held a muffin and a pat of butter. Her shoulders relaxed. "This one is fresh out of the oven. It's still warm. And it's on me. Thank you for not citing me last night."

"Aw. Well now, if that ain't sweeter than Meemaw's peach pudding!"

Shelby held up a hand. "Save your Southernisms. Enjoy the muffin."

She disappeared again into the kitchen. Damon set about making his coffee drinkable. A heaping spoonful of sugar and a handful of flavored creamers usually did the trick. He wondered if he could order tea here without being laughed at. Speaking of tea . . . did they even have sweet tea in Maine? Probably not. Maybe he could suggest it.

The bell above the door rang, signaling new customers. Damon turned his head and raised a hand in greeting to a trio of middle-aged men who took seats at the other end of the counter. "Howdy! Nice mornin', right?"

The men narrowed their eyes and nodded at him.

Sadie pushed through the kitchen doors and set out three mugs in front of the men. "Damon, meet some of the regulars. George, Al, and Simon are lobstermen. Guys, meet Damon Saunders."

George nodded at Damon. "Morning." He turned to Sadie. "They hire him to replace Will? Where's he from?"

"Yep. Damon was a detective in Atlanta."

Al gave him an appraising look. "How did they convince you to move here?" He turned to Simon on his other side. "He might rethink that move come winter."

Simon snorted. "Maybe. Nice to have some new blood in town, though."

Damon flinched. The men were talking about him instead

of to him. "I heard 'bout the opening last month while I was here for my cousin's wedding. Sounded like a nice change of pace."

"I'm sure it is," George said. "Biggest excitement you might get is moose holding up traffic."

Sadie shot him a look of warning. "Not funny, George."

"Oh, right. Yeah." George looked chagrined.

Damon chuckled. "Sounds more exciting than a gator."

The men blinked at him. *Ba dum bum.* Sadie noticed the awkward moment and smiled, but he was sure it was just to be kind. *Different sense of humor here.*

"Let me get you guys some breakfast," she said. "Your usuals?"

The men nodded, and Sadie shot Damon an apologetic smile.

He stared at the kitchen door, willing Shelby to come out.

A moment later, she did. "Hey, guys. I see you've met my friend, Damon." She glanced at him with a small smile. "Now don't go giving him any trouble."

Simon grinned. "Aw, Shelby. You're no fun."

"Ain't that the truth." She set three ramekins of butter on the counter, one in front of each man. "I'm serious. He's new in town, and you best make him feel welcome—or don't expect any of the extras you're accustomed to from me." She lifted her eyebrows to reinforce her words and disappeared back into the kitchen.

Damon grinned. He wondered how he could get her to treat *him* like an old friend, or more, without coming on too strong.

Sadie breezed out a few minutes later with Damon's

breakfast and cheese rolls for the lobstermen. "Top you off?" she asked, glancing at his mug.

"No, thanks." He inhaled deeply and met her eyes. "So how does one go about getting a singing gig at Pastor Porter's church?"